FIXIN' TO GET KILLED

Panic-stricken, the bandit stared at the two Americans and then started to get to his feet. Sergeant Garrity lashed out with the barrel of his Henry, knocking the desperado to the ground.

"Where's the American girl?" he demanded.

The bandit sat up, rubbing his arm. "I don't know nothing about no 'merican *muchacha*."

Without realizing it himself, Lieutenant Boothe suddenly moved. He kicked the bandit in the stomach, pulled his hunting knife from its scabbard, and said, "The American woman is my wife."

The bandit swallowed. "I guess you want her back, eh?"

Boothe bent down and pressed the sharp blade against the man's throat.

"Tell me where to find her or I'll cut your goddamned throat!"

BLOOD OF APACHE MESA

Patrick E. Andrews

ZEBRA BOOKS
KENSINGTON PUBLISHING CORP.

ZEBRA BOOKS

are published by

Kensington Publishing Corp.
475 Park Avenue South
New York, NY 10016

First printing: December, 1988

Printed in the United States of America

Dedicated to
Old Sergeants Everywhere

CHAPTER 1

Quartermaster Sergeant Tom Mulvaney, working on the regimental property book, looked up when he heard the crate crash to the ground outside. Muttering angrily to himself, the N.C.O. laid his pen down and walked from his office to the warehouse dock. A splintered wooden box lay on the ground, its contents of hardtack spilled out into the dirt.

"All right! Which one o' you dolts dropped it?" Mulvaney demanded.

The half-dozen soldiers working on the unloading detail looked at the N.C.O. with expressions of angelic innocence.

"Sure now, do you all want a bit of extra duty then?" Mulvaney asked glaring.

Still no one said a word until a grizzled professional private named Dortmann stepped forward. "I done it, Sergeant Mulvaney." He shrugged. "What the hell difference does it make? You couldn't bust 'em crackers if you rolled this wagon over 'em."

"They're U.S. Army property," Mulvaney pointed out. "Now get the hammer out of the tool shed and put that box together. Mind you brush the dirt off that hardtack too. There ain't a post bakery here, so it's the closest thing to bread we got."

Fort MacNeil, Texas, was a primitive garrison. One end of the warehouse where Mulvaney and the men worked was also used as the regimental headquarters. It was the only permanent building, having been constructed of lumber laboriously hauled down from the Red River Station.

Mulvaney delayed his return to the office long enough to give a warning look at the others to make sure they fully appreciated his concern for items on the official supply lists. He went back inside once more to devote his attention to the supply document. He'd no sooner settled in to the complicated chore of bringing it up to date when he was interrupted again by noise outside.

"Atten-*hut!*"

"God!" the sergeant groaned. Now some officer had shown up in the middle of all the work that had to be done. Mulvaney once again went outside to see which ranker had suddenly appeared. He saw young 2d Lt. Wildon Boothe from L Troop returning Trooper Dortmann's salute. Boothe was a pleasant-looking, blond youngster with an aristocratic face. The officer glanced up at the dock and saw Mulvaney. "Good afternoon, Sergeant."

"Good afternoon, sir. Is there something I could be doing for you?"

Boothe stepped up onto the dock. "Yes. I've come to see about drawing some furniture for my quarters." He had only recently arrived in the regiment and had been billeted with the other bachelor subalterns in their dormitory-like quarters at the end of officers' row.

"Ah, yes, sir," Mulvaney said, suddenly remembering. "Your missus will be joining you soon."

"That's right," Boothe said. "I have to set up suitable quarters before she gets here,"

"Well, not to worry, sir," Mulvaney assured him. "We have some things you can put to good use."

It wasn't army policy to provide furnishings for officers, but on the frontier special provisions had been made due to the difficulty of transportation and purchase of new household items. Officers newly assigned or on temporary duty could be provided for from the quartermaster stores when the necessary things were available.

The sergeant led Boothe toward the rear of the building. They stepped in a corner of the warehouse where some miscellaneous pieces of furniture were stacked. "Not bad, hey, sir?"

Boothe said nothing. There was a battered wooden table, some unmatched straight chairs, a bed that looked as though it had been handmade, and some shelves that also seemed to have been banged together from used boards. "This is all you have?" he asked.

"Yes, sir," Mulvaney answered. "And it's plenty grand for two people."

"Where did this come from?" Boothe asked, clearly disappointed.

"Why from that ranch family that was killed by the Indians last spring," Mulvaney said, confused by the young officer's apparent lack of enthusiasm. "We tried to find their next-of-kin, but it was impossible. So the poor folks' belongings became the official property of the army."

"I suppose it will have to do until we can order some of our own," Boothe said.

"I've got a detail outside unloading wagons now, sir," Mulvaney said. "I'll have 'em tote the goods over to your new quarters."

"Yes, thank you," Boothe said. "I shall meet them there, Sergeant."

Mulvaney opened the front door for the officer. "Now don't you worry none, Lieutenant Boothe. Your bride is gonna love the stuff. Why, it's a grand way to start out an army marriage." He let Boothe out, then walked back to the rear of the loading dock. He stopped outside. "Dortmann! Get these lads up here. You've some lovely furniture to carry over to Lieutenant Boothe's new quarters."

"Can we use the wagon, Sergeant?" Trooper Dortmann asked.

"And put extra use on it? No!" Mulvaney barked.

Dortmann grinned and pointed to his boots. "We'll wear our footgear out."

"I might have you do it barefoot, bucko!" Mulvaney snapped. "Now get up here!"

While the soldiers prepared to transport the furniture, Boothe walked across the post to his new quarters. He looked at the small house made of sod blocks. Although the window frames were wood and had glass in them, the roof was no more than a tarpaulin especially cut for its function. Sighing inwardly, he opened the door. Even though it had been freshly swept and dusted, it still looked like the inside of a large, empty henhouse to him.

* * *

It was the autumn of 1883, and the year had been

an exciting one for 2d Lt. Wildon Boothe of the United States Cavalry. That spring the young scion of a wealthy upstate New York family had graduated from the U.S. Military Academy at West Point to fulfill a lifelong dream.

Wildon had always wanted to be a soldier. An uncle had raised a volunteer infantry regiment to serve the Union cause during the Civil War at about the time Wildon was born. As the youngster grew up, he was regaled with tales of glory about fierce battles in such places as Manassas, Antietam, and Gettysburg. Even after the war the uncle maintained his service in the state militia, and Wildon loved to be allowed to attend muster days when the part-time soldiers gathered for parades, drills, and camping in tents at the Catskill military reservation. When he was twelve, he was given a gift that was to be the favorite of his boyhood: a cut-down uniform just like the ones the militiamen wore.

The boy's other valued playthings were his toy soldiers, wooden rifles, and other martial toys. As he grew older, books on military subjects and wars became an obsession with him. No one was surprised when he asked his uncle's aid in procuring a congressional appointment to West Point.

In his later teens, before attending the academy, two more interests appeared in his life. An active, athletic youngster in spite of his slim build, he loved horseback riding and hunting. The two pastimes were a passion with him, and he developed into a skilled equestrian and a dead shot.

Horseback riding, however, introduced the young man to an even deeper preoccupation. This was Hes-

11

ter Bristol. Three years younger than Wildon, she was the heiress of the Bristol Soap fortune and came from a family as socially prominent as Wildon's. She, too, loved to ride. Hating the constrictions of sidesaddles, she was known to impetuously mount a horse with a regular saddle and gallop, with stockinged legs showing above her boots, across the rolling terrain to take jumps over fences, creeks, and other obstacles. Actually, she and Wildon had known each other as small children, but only when they were older did they develop any real affection, which manifested itself through their common interest in horses. Later, those feelings became romantic and loving, and Wildon's awkward attentions at dances and parties evolved into serious courtship. The evening before he left for West Point, their engagement was announced.

A month after Wildon's graduation from the military academy, they were married in one of the season's most prominent weddings at Hester's family estate on Lake Champlain. After a short honeymoon at Niagara Falls, the young couple was separated while the brand-new second lieutenant went west to join his cavalry regiment at Fort MacNeil in central Texas. The plan was for Hester to wait at her family's home until he had managed to settle in and could send for her. Neither of the young people realized what was in store for them out in the desolate frontier country.

Wildon knew the cavalry forts were not elegant, unlike the Eastern garrisons. He had heard a bit from soldiers who had served in the West, and an occasional officer detached from a frontier unit

12

would be assigned to West Point as an instructor. Yet he still did not fully appreciate the tough conditions endured by soldiers in the Indian campaigns. He thought it would be rather like the militia camps with a few tents and perhaps with well-constructed frame buildings.

Hester, on the other hand, was in complete ignorance of the army's situation. The only military post she had ever seen was West Point during visits with her mother to see Wildon. In her mind, all garrisons were constructed of gray granite buildings and well-kept green parade grounds within the dignified protection of stone walls.

When Wildon arrived at Fort MacNeil, he was appalled at what he saw. The officers' quarters were no more than sod huts with canvas roofs. They were filthy, insect-infested, and crude beyond imagination, and he had stared at them in near shock. A dearth of building materials made it impossible to build anything better.

He was also unpleasantly surprised at the enlisted men he soon commanded. A large percentage were foreign-born, including a few who could hardly understand English. Many of the Americans were rejects from society with tendencies toward crime, dirtiness, and insubordination. Others were naive youngsters looking for adventure, who soon had such boyish ideas pushed out of their heads by endless drill, hard physical labor, and the unbelievable tedium of being stationed far from any of civilization's amenities and pleasures.

The noncommissioned officers included brutes who kept order and discipline through painful physical punishments, kicks and beatings, and abject fear. Wildon was quick to learn that this kind of sergeant and corporal was necessary to keep the majority of troopers under any kind of control.

But the one thing that the socially segregated officers, noncommissioned officers, and soldiers all shared in common was a marked tendency to drink strong liquor in large quantities. Drunkenness was everywhere to an extent that shocked a properly raised New Englander from a wealthy, cultured, and socially conscious family.

Yet Wildon's love of soldiering was such that he quickly adapted to the situation. He was a young man with a hard, realistic way of looking at things. The army wasn't supposed to be a soft life, and even his uncle had warned him that enlisted men in the regular army were certainly not like the citizen-soldiers of the militia. It was a tough job requiring tough men. In order to be a good officer, Wildon would be expected to endure unpleasantness and inconvenience in both garrison and the field with the same fortitude he would be required to display toward danger in war. His healthy emotional outlook helped him to accept the hard realities of the Regular Army as a challenge. Within a few weeks he had settled in quite well.

One other aspect of the life at the desolate garrison — besides the martial pomp and ceremony — Wildon found to his complete liking: plenty of opportunity for hunting on the wild prairie. Game in the form of buffalo, antelope, elk, and deer were abundant. Wildon never missed a chance to join a group of fellow officers for a shooting trip to bag fresh game for the mess halls. He even followed his companions' example by purchasing a buckskin outfit complete with broad-brimmed hat for the pastime.

But Wildon knew such recreation would not amuse Hester. After some long, serious thought, he decided that the blunt truth was the best course to follow. He wrote Hester a painfully detailed description of Fort MacNeil. He told of the officers' quarters, the soldiers, the hard drinking, and even of the several uncouth characters in the officer cadre. He sent the letter with the full realization that his beloved might decide to stay back in New York or insist that he leave the army and return home to her.

But Hester's reaction surprised him. She responded to the letter with a girlish, romantic reply saying she would go anywhere her true love must go. She even added an innocent postscript saying she thought the whole affair would be a wonderful and grand adventure.

Wildon knew that attitude would be dashed to pieces within the first five minutes she spent at Fort MacNeil.

Trooper Dortmann banged on the door. "Sir! We're here with the furniture."

"Yes. Come in," Wildon responded.

"Any place in particular you want it?" Dortmann asked as he and the others struggled into the small room.

Wildon looked around. "The tables and chairs can stay in here. Take the bed and those shelves into the other room."

It didn't take the soldiers long to put the sparse furnishings into place. Dortmann, who was the senior private present, was a member of Wildon's troop. "There you are, sir. All settled in."

"Yes, thank you. Dismissed. But I would like a word with you, Trooper Dortmann," Wildon said.

"Yes, sir."

The young officer waited for the others to go outside. "You're a veteran soldier, aren't you?"

"Ten years of service, sir."

"A man with your experience would serve the army better as a noncommissioned officer," Wildon said bluntly. "I would recommend that you apply yourself a bit harder to earn some chevrons for your sleeves."

"No, thank you, sir," Dortmann replied cheerfully. "I like being a private soljer, sir. In all this time, I've never had as much as a lance jack's stripes to boast of. And I like it that way."

"I see," Wildon said. "Very well. You're dismissed." He realized his uncle had been entirely correct. There were types of soldiers in the Regular Army that would never be found in a gentleman's militia regiment. He was disappointed in Dortmann, but his more pressing problems came back to mind once more.

Turning around, Wildon could see that the place actually looked worse with the awful table and chairs. He walked over and sat down in one of them, knowing that the first crisis in his marriage would begin the instant Hester walked into their new home.

CHAPTER 2

A balmy breeze wafted off Lake Champlain, rippling the silk curtains as it made its way with gentle persistence to float through the room. The sweet smells it gathered off the garden added to the pleasure of the early afternoon's warmth.

Hester Bristol Boothe, wife of 2d Lt. Wildon Boothe, turned from the open window and looked at her cousin Penelope and sister Fionna. Both were gently repacking her things into the large hope chest. Hester was a small young woman of eighteen years, trim and graceful, her long brown tresses held in place with a silver comb. Slightly freckled across the bridge of her small nose, she had laughing green eyes and a full mouth that smiled easily.

"I can't believe it," Hester said. "It seems so unreal now that I'm leaving."

She looked once again out across the rose garden. These were the Ellsworth variety. Her father took so much pride in them that he wouldn't permit even the family gardener to touch his beloved plants. The flowers grew abundantly and beautifully in the late summer sunshine. This fragrant area was tucked in behind a high brick wall. From that point, a well-cared-for lawn sloped down toward the lakeshore.

Penelope looked up at Hester. "Why don't you stop gawking out the window and help us?"

Hester smirked. "It was your idea to take everything out of the chest and look at it. So it's only fair for you to put it back. And don't you dare break any of my things! Maybe I should call Ethel to do it."

"No!" Penelope pleaded. "We'll be careful, Hester."

"It's fun!" Fionna exclaimed in her fourteen-year-old enthusiasm. "Just think! You won't be taking these things out until you're far away in Texas."

"With your true love," Penelope added.

"Ooh! I'm going to marry an army officer too," Fionna said. She sighed. "And in the West Point chapel like you did, Hester."

"That shouldn't be a big surprise," Penelope said. "You fell in love with every cadet you saw."

"So did you," Fionna said.

"Well—maybe," Penelope said. The three girls laughed. "Actually," she said as an afterthought, "unless you really know and recognize one of them, they all look alike."

"That's what's fun," Hester said. "Knowing one of them."

"I think the best part of the whole wedding was when you left the church," Fionna said. "It looked so elegant with those officers making an arch of their swords while you and Wildon walked under them. You were like a prince and princess."

"That's how I felt," Hester said. "I was with my

handsome prince."

"Wildon is handsome, isn't he?" Fionna said.

"He's certainly skinny though," Penelope remarked.

"But he is still handsome!" Hester said almost angrily. "Or I wouldn't have married him. He looks grand sitting a horse too."

Penelope looked at Fionna. "That's why she married him. He likes to ride."

"Yes," Fionna agreed.

"Common interests make a strong marriage," Hester preached. "Besides, you must admit he was the most dashing cadet at West Point."

Penelope took a neatly folded stack of petticoats and carefully placed them in the trunk. "What's the place you're going to like?"

"It must be marvelous," Hester said. "Wildon described it to me in a letter. He said it was very rustic, not at all like West Point. He said they actually had buildings made of squares of dirt."

"Dirt?" Fionna asked. "Real dirt?"

"Yes. They're called 'soddies' by everyone out there," Hester said. "And they have canvas for roofs."

"Oooh!" Penelope said with a wince. "Is that how you're going to live, Hester?"

"Oh, of course not! That's just Wildon's little joke," Hester said. "I've already seen how officers and their ladies live at West Point." She smiled. "But I played along with his silly jest. I wrote and told him I thought it would be a great adventure to live in a dirt house."

"Wildon will have to get up pretty early in the

morning to fool you, Hester," her sister said. "So what sort of home will you have?"

"Well, I know it won't be as nice as the older officer's houses," Hester admitted. "I imagine we'll be in a cottage or something."

"With vines all around it?" Fionna asked. "And flowers?"

"Roses," Hester decided. "There shall be roses, but not as nice as Father's, of course."

"They wouldn't dare be," Penelope said. "Not even in the army."

The trio laughed again.

"Did Wildon tell you about the wild Indians?" Fionna asked.

"Oh, yes," Hester answered. "He said there were thousands of them and that they attack the fort every day at three o'clock sharp."

"Hester!" the two other girls called out.

She smiled. "He said there were only a few. The bad ones are far away from Fort MacNeil. He said the fighting had all but ended in that area."

"I suppose he was disappointed," Penelope said.

"Oh, yes. In fact, he said there really isn't much for the soldiers to do."

"Thank goodness," Penelope said. "At least we won't have to worry about you."

Hester looked around the room. "I'm going to miss this place."

"You'd better take a good look around while you have the chance," Penelope warned her.

"Yes! You'll be leaving tomorrow," Fionna emphasized. "And you probably won't be back for years and years."

The conversation was abruptly interrupted by the appearance of Hester's mother in the doorway of the room. She came in, moving gracefully for a woman who could kindly be described as full-figured. "Girls! What in the world are you doing? You've taken everything out of the hope chest."

"They're putting it back, Mother," Hester said. "Don't worry."

"I think it best that Ethel take care of that," Mrs. Bristol said.

"Mother!" Fionna exclaimed. "We're perfectly capable of handling this."

"Just do it with care—a lot of care," Mrs. Bristol said. She slipped a pudgy arm around Hester. "I must talk to you a moment, dear. I know this is an awkward time, but everything is so hectic right now."

"Yes, Mother."

"Out on the balcony." Mrs. Bristol looked over at Fionna and Penelope. "Excuse us for a few moments, dears."

The two stepped through the double doors. The view before them was a beautiful combination of rose garden, lawn, and the shore of Lake Champlain. The quiet added to the charm of the vista. Hester suddenly felt very sentimental. "This is a beautiful home," she said.

The mother embraced the daughter. "I hate to think of you leaving it."

"In a way I do too," Hester admitted. "But what is it you wanted to tell me?"

"You know, of course, that Albert and Ethel are going along to see you safely to that place in Texas." She referred to the married couple that had been

21

employed by the family for more than twenty years.

"Yes, Mother. We discussed that ages ago," Hester said, complaining good-naturedly. "Now what do you really want to talk about? You never come right out and speak up."

"I want you to remember that you're a Bristol and always will be in spite of your married name," Mrs. Bristol said. "Your conduct will reflect greatly on the family."

"Do you think I'll do something to disgrace us?" Hester asked mischievously. "Now, please, Mother! Say whatever it is you wish to say."

"Hester, you're such a tomboy!" her mother exclaimed. "I don't want you to forget to always ride sidesaddle. Those army ladies are a snobbish bunch for some unfathomable reason. They'll be watching you closely."

"Mother—"

"Hush! You have a tendency to get overexuberant at times," Mrs. Bristol continued. "You must control those feelings and be more demure. I am fully aware that you have ridden with an English saddle and raced around with your limbs exposed," she chided her. "We can't have any more of that."

Hester rolled her eyes.

"Now let's consider your hiring of a domestic," Mrs. Bristol said. "We'll be sending you money, of course."

"Of course," Hester said. "Wildon gets some sort of trust fund thing from his family too. He says we could never live properly on an army officer's pay."

"Why, of why, did that boy decide to go into the army?" Mrs. Bristol wondered aloud. "He could get a nice position in his father's business or in ours if he wished."

"Everybody knows that Wildon has always been addle-brained about soldiers," Hester said. "It's quite all right with me."

"Never mind, dear. Will you need Albert or Ethel's help in engaging a maid? Remember they are quite proficient in that."

"I shall take care of the matter myself," Hester said.

Mrs. Bristol displayed an expression of concern. "Are you happy, dear?"

"Yes, Mother. I love Wildon with all my heart."

"I know," Mrs. Bristol said. She hugged her daughter. "Fine. Now let's go back inside." She led her daughter through the doors to rejoin Fionna and Penelope. After taking time to warn them once again to take care of the repacking, the woman left the girls alone.

Fionna smiled. "Was Mother her old self?"

"Of course," Hester said with a sigh. "I was told to be ladylike and was given some advice." She walked to the room's largest window, and gazed fondly out over what had been her home her entire life. The Bristol estate was located among the choicest acreage along Lake Champlain's shores. Her grandfather had made the family fortune with Bristol Soap, a fragrant ladies' brand that was advertised daily on the front page of every major metropolitan newspaper in the East:

As Delicate as the Lady Who Uses it — Bristol Soap for Madame and Mademoiselle.

23

Penelope interrupted Hester's reverie. "How long will Albert and Ethel stay with you?"

"Until the next transportation back East," Hester said. "Wildon said he has arranged temporary quarters for them at Fort MacNeil, but the accommodations cannot be held for more than a week or two. It doesn't matter. I shall hire a maid as quickly as possible."

"Why not have Wildon do it?" Fionna asked. "That way you will already have one when you arrive."

"Mother says men are simply awful when it comes to a household staff," Hester said.

"And she's right," Penelope said with the experience of seventeen years of servant-filled living behind her.

"Once, awhile back, she even made a list of things I should look for," Hester said, laughing. "With two of the things to take into consideration being clean fingernails and a wholesome, pale complexion."

"That's not much help if you hire a colored lady," Penelope said.

"Or an Indian squaw," Fionna suggested. "That would be fun."

Penelope laughed aloud. "Squaws don't work as maids, silly!"

"They might out West," Fionna countered.

"Oh, let's talk about other things," Penelope insisted.

"Yes," Fionna agreed. "Will there be many military balls, Hester?"

"There most certainly will," Hester answered.

"That means that Wildon will be dashing in his fancy uniform and I shall wear the latest fashions and cause all the other officers to fall madly in love with me."

"Oh, dear!" Fionna cried. "You won't be a flirt, will you, Hester?"

"Of course," Hester said. "And an outrageous one at that."

"You had better be careful," Penelope warned her. She packed away several sheets, the last of the contents of the hope chest.

Hester felt uncertain. "Perhaps I should have Ethel come and repack everything."

"Hester!" Penelope exclaimed in girlish exasperation. "We can do this job quite well, thank you." She paused thoughtfully. "As a matter of fact, it wouldn't be a bad idea if we began putting things in your trunk and valise now. To save time later on."

"Yes," Hester agreed. "Perhaps we should."

Fionna, who had gone over to the closet, called out to her sister. "How many of these ball gowns are you taking, Hester? Remember Father is going to have most of your things shipped in a month or so."

"Just put in one," Hester said.

Fionna took one and brought it out. She held the dress up. "What about—" She hesitated. "Hester." Suddenly the younger girl burst into tears. "Oh, Hester! I shall miss you terribly!"

Hester walked over and embraced her. "And I you, Fionna."

"What about me?" Penelope asked, joining them. The trio had been avoiding the reality of the situation. Hester was going to go a long distance away, and there was every possibility that it would be years before they saw each other again.

All three stood tightly entwined, sobbing softly.

CHAPTER 3

The fifty men of Troop L were seated tall in their saddles, ready to go through a mounted inspection. Because this was no full-dress affair, they sported their second-best military finery.

Used to the pomp and strict protocol of West Point, 2d Lt. Wildon Boothe felt a stab of disapproval as he turned to catch a quick glimpse of the enlisted troopers behind him. Although all were in regulation garrison uniform of kepi, blouse, trousers, boots, and leather accouterments that Quartermaster Sergeant Mulvaney had issued, they were still not dressed in a completely similar manner. Several of the horse soldiers were attired in yellow-trimmed, short jackets of the type used during the Civil War that had ended eighteen years previously. A few more of the troopers were clad in the longer sackcloth coat model of 1872, and others had the later style which were of the same cut, but were piped with yellow cord around the collar and edge of the cuffs.

Wildon consoled himself with the thought that at least these were real professional soldiers of the Regular Army. Perhaps if a tight-fisted Congress loosened up some military purse strings, not only could the men of the regiment be clothed alike, but their worn field gear could be replaced by new haversacks, cartridge belts, and canteens.

The troop commander, Capt. Fred Armbrewster, drew his saber. "Prepare for inspection! March, front!" He was a paunchy officer in his late forties. Although not a dashing figure, he performed the rituals of both mounted and dismounted drill perfectly. Even Wildon, after four years of parade ground ceremonies at West Point, could find no fault in the other officer's execution of military marching.

The guidon bearer and bugler moved smartly into proper position. Since this was a mounted inspection, the carbines were not going to be looked at. Only pistols and sabers. The captain turned his horse with Wildon, the troop's only other officer, following him. As they passed each man, the trooper displayed his saber and pistol in the prescribed manner. The captain and lieutenant rode around the troop, then back to the front.

"First Sergeant!" the captain barked.

Sergeant James Garrity, a veteran line noncommissioned officer who was acting as the troop first sergeant, urged his horse a few hoof-clomping steps forward. He saluted sharply.

"Dismiss the troop," Armbrewster commanded.

"Yes, sir."

Wildon and Captain Armbrewster rode off toward the regimental stables. When they reached the building, the two officers dismounted and handed their horses over to a waiting orderly. Armbrewster was in a good mood. "Well, you'll be a regular married man like the rest of us in another couple of days or so, hey, Mister Boothe?"

"Yes, sir," Wildon answered.

The two strolled out of the stable area in casual conversation. But, despite the informality, they still observed military custom. Wildon, as the junior ranking man, walked to Armbrewster's left. Both held their sheathed sabers in the correct manner next to the left leg. This left the right hand free to return the salutes they might receive from any passing enlisted men.

"You haven't forgotten the dinner party at Major Darnell's tonight, have you?" Armbrewster asked.

"No, sir," Wildon answered.

"We'll let Sergeant Garrity handle the retreat formation," Armbrewster said. "We wouldn't want to be late for our squadron commander's soirée, would we?"

"I shall be there, standing tall as a good subaltern."

"Uh, yes, Boothe," Armbrewster said a bit uneasily. "I really must talk to you about something."

"About what, sir?"

"That white mess jacket of yours," Armbrewster said. "It has created quite a stir."

"I had it especially made just before my graduation from the academy, sir," Wildon said. "Actually, it was a gift from my uncle. He is a brigadier general in the New York State Militia."

"Yes, of course, but you see, young man, it is the only such item of uniform on this post," Armbrewster said. "None of the other officers have one. That, unfortunately, includes our own squadron and regimental commanders."

29

Wildon wasn't sure what Armbrewster was getting at. "Yes, sir?"

"Actually, it wouldn't be a very good idea for you to wear it at any future functions, Mister Boothe," Armbrewster said. "I have been specifically instructed to tell you that."

"I'm certainly sorry if I offended—"

"Oh, pshaw, young man!" Armbrewster said with a smile. "There has been no offense taken. And you must take into consideration that it isn't regulation."

"Of course, sir," Wildon said. "Thank you."

"I knew you would understand." They had reached Armbrewster's quarters. "Then I shall see you at Major Darnell's at seven-thirty."

"Yes, sir." Wildon saluted. He walked on down officers' row, feeling a bit embarrassed. He realized he had what was termed in the army as "money on the outside," but he hadn't really given it much thought. Naturally, any officer eking by on only his military pay could never afford a white mess jacket complete with gold lacing on the sleeves. His uncle had spent more on that one piece of apparel than most officers spent on their entire army wardrobe.

Wildon walked down to his own quarters, the last in the row, as was appropriate for the regiment's most subordinate lieutenant, and let himself in. As usual, when he entered the small sod house, he felt a stab of regret.

Hester would never stand for living in such a place.

He hung up his kepi on a hatrack picked up at the sutler's store. After removing his sword belt, he placed the saber there too. Wildon took another look, then walked over to one of the wooden chairs and slumped down in it.

He loved the army. Even after the unhappy introduction to reality at Fort MacNeil, his enthusiasm for military life had not been dampened a whit. Wildon knew he'd wear army blue until he either retired or was laid low by some Indian warrior's bullet. But the stinging knowledge that his wife Hester was going to detest it hung heavy in his heart, taking away what enjoyment he should be experiencing in moving into the regimental environment. When his mind dwelt on the inevitable conflict awaiting him and his wife, his thoughts turned the darkest and most pessimistic. The notes of Retreat sounded by one of the regimental band's trumpeters, snapped him out of his disagreeable lethargy.

Wanting to think of more pleasant things, he stood up and walked over to the built-in cupboard used as a closet. Hanging there among the uniforms was his hunting outfit. He pulled out the buckskin outfit and looked at it. He smiled, thinking of how he would have his picture taken in it the first time a photographer made an appearance at Fort MacNeil. Seeing him dressed up like that would really create a stir back in New York.

Suddenly remembering the time, he went into the other room where the cookstove was located. After lighting the kindling and putting in some small scraps of wood for a small fire to heat the cauldron of water, he dragged the bathtub from its place in the corner to get ready for an evening at Major Darnell's quarters.

After bathing, shaving, and slicking down his hair,

Wildon picked out a uniform. He would really have preferred the mess jacket, but Captain Armbrewster had set him straight. Instead, he chose a normal garrison uniform with dark-blue blouse and light-blue trousers sporting the yellow stripe of the cavalry down each side. He slipped into it, hoping the fact that it was made of expensive material and especially tailored in New York City would not be noticed.

When he was properly prepared, he stepped out of his quarters and walked back up toward the field officers' area. It was a peaceful time of the day. The men, at least those not on guard duty or sentenced as garrison prisoners to extra duty, were in their mess halls. After eating, they would have a few hours of free time. Since there had been a recent payday, most would be at the sutler's getting drunk or playing at any of the numerous illegal card games that seemed to appear mysteriously in out-of-the-way places where it would be difficult for the officer of the day or sergeant of the guard to discover the pastime.

Wildon reached the Darnells' door and knocked. The door was opened by the major's wife, Sophie Darnell, a middle-aged woman who had been an officer's lady for over thirty years. Wildon bowed properly. "My compliments, ma'am."

Mrs. Darnell smiled and stepped back to allow him to enter. "Good evening, Mister Boothe," she said. "Please come in and join us."

"Thank you very much," Wildon said. He'd never noticed the difference between a major's home and a lowly lieutenant's quarters before. More spacious, with superior furniture, it was better constructed and had windows that slid up and down. There was also a fireplace with a mantel. Wildon knew that Hester was going to resent the hell out of that.

"There is punch on the sideboard in the kitchen," Mrs. Darnell informed him. "The gentlemen are out there if you would care to join them."

"Very well," Wildon said.

"You'll be dropping your lady off with us at the next little get-together we have, won't you?" Mrs. Darnell said. "We are all so looking forward to meeting her."

"Yes," Wildon said. He walked through the living room, pausing to politely greet the other wives there. As per protocol, he stopped for a longer pause with his troop commander's wife, Elisa Armbrewster.

Mrs. Armbrewster, the same age as Sophie Darnell, also felt inclined to speak of Hester's pending arrival. "Mister Boothe, we are so anxious to meet your lady. Especially since she's from the East."

"Yes, Mrs. Armbrewster," Wildon said. "New York State to be exact."

"She'll think we're such frumps," Mrs. Armbrewster said, feigning a frown. "We're so out of date."

"I'm sure she'll find you as charming as I have," Wildon said, not wanting to get into any prolonged conversation about Hester.

"At least she'll brighten up our drab existence here," Mrs. Armbrewster insisted.

Wildon was rescued by a call from the kitchen. "Mister Boothe!" It was Major Darnell. "Come join the men. Don't become a prisoner of war of the ladies."

"It is a captivity I would not mind enduring," Wildon said.

"Why, Mister Boothe!" Mrs. Armbrewster declared. "That's another nice thing you've said since you came in the door. First you say you found us charming, now you willingly surrender to us ladies."

"Yes, ma'am," Wildon said. "Please excuse me."

"Ah, yes!" Mrs. Armbrewster said in understanding. "The major summons you!"

Wildon joined the other officers. He liked the rough male camaraderie he experienced in the regiment. The others were off to one side of the room happily indulging in guzzling down the heavily spiked punch. Besides Major Darnell and Captain Armbrewster, there were two more troop commanders, and the regimental surgeon.

Darnell, a bit drunk, roared out in laughter. "Well, young Mister Boothe, are you enjoying your final carefree days of bachelorhood?"

"Yes, sir," Wildon answered with a broad grin. He got himself a cupful of the drink.

The surgeon, an alcoholic named Dempster, was already weaving slightly. "And how soon will I be delivering any little Boothes?"

"I can't say, sir," Wildon said. "I think I must concentrate on her introduction to army life before seriously thinking of raising a family." He looked over to the other side of the room and saw two self-conscious mess cooks preparing the dinner. They kept their heads down in a mute pretense that they weren't really observing the officers getting drunk. Wildon knew the soldiers were actually enjoying the experience and would spread tales in the barracks that same evening.

Armbrewster nudged the surgeon. "Go on with

34

your story, old man."

"Huh? Oh, yeah," Dempster said. "So this soldier came in on sick call complaining of a—" He glanced at the door to make sure none of the ladies was near. "—dripping member. So I examined him, and it didn't take me long to figure out what was wrong. 'Trooper,' says I, 'you got—'" Another look at the door. "'—you got the clap and I'm going to have to write you up on it.' So he asked me what would happen to him, and I told him they'd put him in the guardhouse for three months."

"What'd he say 'bout that?" Darnell asked in a slurred voice.

"He said, 'Sir, not that! I can't pull three months in the guardhouse,'" The surgeon chuckled again. "So I says to him, 'Well, trooper *pull* what you can and *push* the rest'!"

Wildon liked the story. That really sounded Regular Army to him. He held onto his drink and joined his fellow officers as they dissolved into gales of drunken laughter.

CHAPTER 4

Wildon walked out the main gate and looked down the road into the distance. He stared through the dancing heat haze for long minutes before walking back into the shade provided by the post stables.

The young lieutenant was waiting for the arrival of the stagecoach on which his wife and her two servants were riding. Although there was no town near Fort MacNeil, it was located on the stage line between Red River Station and Dallas. The company that ran the transportation service was under contract to carry mail and passengers for the army.

The four soldiers who had been detailed to help with the luggage lounged nearby, glad for the opportunity to get away from the drill for the morning. Trooper Gus Dortmann and his friend Trooper John Jones watched bemused at the young officer's impatience. "It must be wonderful to be in love," Dortmann whispered with a wink to Jones.

Jones nodded. He'd served in another regiment under his real name a few years earlier. Kicked out of the army with a bad-conduct "bobtail" discharge, he had reenlisted under a new identity after nearly starving to death in the civilian world. When he'd

36

made his fraudulent second entry in the army, he'd said his name was John Smith. The recruiting sergeant told him that the monthly quota of "John Smiths" had already been used up. Not being too imaginative, Jones then announced his name as John Jones.

Dortmann spat a stream of tobacco juice. "Wait'll she starts nagging him about his drinking," he said. "The lieutenant will be trying to get her to go back East."

"Aw," Jones said. "The kid don't drink hardly at all. I know that for a fact."

"Give him another coupla years out here," Dortmann said. "He'll be a John Barleycorn officer for sure." He pointed at Wildon going back for another look. "Yeah, he's impatient all right. We've been waiting for two hours now."

"So what?" Jones asked. "It sure beats hell out of drill call or stable call, don't it?" He pointed over at the other two soldiers napping by the stable. "They sure ain't complaining."

"Dortmann!" Wildon's voice interrupted the conversation.

"Yes, sir?"

"Here comes the stagecoach. Get the men out here."

"Yes, sir!" Dortmann walked over and gave the sleeping troopers a couple of light kicks. "C'mon. It's time to tote for the new officer's lady."

The two troopers, yawning and stretching, got to their feet. Both were young, in their late teens. "I didn't join the army to carry folks' luggage," the one named Rampey said.

"Me either," his companion Mauson added with an undisguised tone of resentment in his voice.

Dortmann sneered. "What the hell did you 'list up for? To fight Injuns?"

"Yeah!" Rampey said in youthful defiance.

"Well, you got in the wrong regiment, boys. There ain't a riled-up redskin closer'n Fort Sill," Jones said.

"And even if there was hostiles, you'd still be toting for the officers," Dortmann said. "Now let's go and be nice about it."

The stage had been so far away when Wildon sighted it that the conveyance didn't reach them for a half-hour. When it did, the attitude of the driver and guard showed they weren't planning on tarrying. One tossed down valises from the top of the stage, while the other went around the back to unbuckle the straps on the rear boot. He was a feisty old man with a droopy gray mustache. He glanced over at the soldiers. "Let's go, soljer boys. We ain't got all day."

Dortmann and Jones saw to it that the youngsters were the ones to handle the heavy stuff. Rampey and Mauson walked over and wrestled Hester's heavy hope chest off the coach.

Meanwhile Wildon held the door and helped Hester down to the road. He had not seen her in months, having only a photograph to remind him of her beauty. She seemed to have grown even lovelier, but he could easily detect her fatigue and irritation despite the smile she gave him.

"Hester, dearest!" he said.

"Oh, Wildon, I'm here at last!" she said almost desperately.

She was followed by Albert and Ethel. Albert, an

38

old family retainer, was scarecrow thin with a hawkish face that also showed the strain of the journey. Ethel, appearing to be on the verge of exhaustion and collapse, lowered herself down from the conveyance and reeled about, hanging onto Wildon for support.

"Master Wildon!" she gasped. "Oh, Master Wildon!"

Albert, stern and tired, merely executed a slight bow. "I shall see to the luggage, sir."

"Thank you, Albert," Wildon said. "I have brought four soldiers to help."

Hester looked over at the men picking up their belongings. They certainly were not like the ones in the garrison detachment she'd seen at West Point. These fellows were unkempt and even a bit surly. The soldiers stationed in the garrison at the military academy had always been lively and eager to please.

Within a few moments, the group trooped through the main gate and across the parade ground toward officers' row. Wildon braced himself for the inevitable when he reached his quarters. He paused and pushed the door open. "Here we are."

Albert stepped back a pace. "Is this where Ethel and I are to stay?"

"No," Wildon answered with a weak grin. "I've arranged for a tent to be pitched for you." He motioned to the soldiers. "Take it all inside, men." As the soldiers carted the stuff in, the others remained outside.

Hester smiled weakly. "I don't understand, Wildon. What is this place?"

"It is our home, Hester dear."

"Wildon, it is made of dirt."

He nodded. "Yes. Remember my letter? I told you all about it. You said it would be a grand adventure."

Hester waited for the soldiers to come back outside. Then she entered through the door.

Wildon turned to Dortmann. "Take Albert and Ethel to the tent behind the N.C.O. quarters. Then you can dismiss the men."

"Yes, sir," Dortmann said saluting. "C'mon, folks."

Wildon went inside and found Hester standing in the middle of the room. "Do we live here, Wildon?"

"Yes," Wildon said. "It's not much, but we really haven't had time to purchase the things we need. We have three rooms, Hester. This is the parlor and dining room."

Hester looked at the table and three mismatched chairs. "All in one room?"

"Yes, dear. The next room is our bedroom."

When they went into the sleeping quarters, Hester looked at the homemade bed. "Is this all the furniture in here? No bedstands?" She glanced around in a desperate fashion. "No closets! Wildon, there are no closets!"

He pointed to the cupboard covered by a curtain. "That serves as the closet, darling. I can arrange to have another constructed by one of the men. It would be ready in a couple of weeks. The kitchen is through here." He wanted to keep the tour and led her into a room that was bare except for a cookstove.

"Wildon, the bedroom is between our kitchen and dining room," Hester pointed out. "The maid will have to walk through our boudoir in order to serve us."

"Uh, yes, Hester," Wildon said. "I must tell you about that. There is no domestic help available at the moment."

"Wildon!"

"There are no nearby towns, Hester," Wildon explained. "And all of the married enlisted men's wives are already engaged."

"We must speak more of this," Hester said.

"Now, the back yard is right out here."

Hester numbly followed him outside. She looked at the privy and said nothing.

Wildon pointed to the water barrel by the door. "A detail of soldiers comes around regularly and fills it up." He grinned. "All you can drink."

"Really, Wildon. I—" Her shriek was so loud it echoed several times off into the empty prairie.

The rattlesnake in the back yard, surprised and angry, coiled up and prepared to defend itself. Wildon pulled her back inside, then retrieved his saber from its sheath on the clothes rack. He went back into the yard. After a few moments, he returned. "They're a diamondback variety," he said. "Very similar to our timber rattlers in New York."

"The snakes in New York do not come up to one's back door, Wildon," Hester said. "They wouldn't dare!"

"Indeed not," Wildon said. They went back to the living room portion of the small house. "You must realize that these quarters are for second lieutenants. After I am promoted, we shall be able to move into somewhat—" He wanted to use the right words. "—

grander quarters, Hester dear."

Hester sat down in one of the chairs. "How soon, Wildon, will you be advanced?"

"I should make first lieutenant in about ten years."

"Ten years!"

"How was your trip, Hester?" he asked abruptly, wanting to close that area of conversation.

She gritted her teeth. "It was ghastly. There were ruffians all over the place. Most seemed to find singular delight in tormenting poor Albert."

"He is a funny old bird," Wildon pointed out not too wisely. He immediately changed the subject again when he saw her reaction. "I've purchased some plates and cups from the sutler's store. Knives and forks too. They're not very fancy, but they'll do nicely until we can get some better things."

Hester began to weep. Each sob took her deeper into despair until the tears flowed copiously. Wretched, tired, unhappy, and horribly disappointed, she let her trampled emotions pour out without restraint.

Wildon did his best to soothe her jangled feelings. Although awkward and inexperienced at such an undertaking, he succeeded more from Hester's love for him than from any real comfort he was able to give.

An hour later Albert and Ethel returned from their tent. Their mood had not improved in the slightest. It was easy to tell that it was only with a great effort that they had managed to make themselves available for service that evening. Wildon tried to make light of the situation.

"I'm sorry about the tent," he said. "But there were absolutely no permanent buildings available as visitors' quarters."

Ethel looked around the sod house. "That's quite all right, Master Wildon. We'll make do."

"It's only for a few days," Albert said. He closed his eyes as if praying. "Then we shall return to the East."

"I shall see to dinner," Ethel said. She glanced around. "The kitchen?"

"Through the bedroom," Wildon said.

"The bedroom, sir?" Albert asked.

"Yes. But I'm afraid there's nothing but salt pork and canned peaches. It was all the sutler has had for a while. I do have some coffee purchased from the quartermaster, however."

It was not necessary for Albert, his nose wrinkling with distaste, to express his feelings. He motioned to Ethel. "Come, my dear."

Less than a half-hour later, Wildon and Hester sat down to their first meal in the new house. Served on plain, white platters, the food stood out starkly. Hester didn't eat much, but Wildon's appetite was in top form. He took a bite of salt pork and chewed thoughtfully. "You might be interested to know," he said to Hester, "that we shall be able to buy vegetables from the company garden."

"Really?" Hester asked in a weak voice.

"Oh, yes. We have one of the soldiers permanently detailed as a gardener," Wildon said. "It's very important work. Without it, there would be no greens to eat."

Hester was in no mood for small talk. "Wildon, without domestic help, we shall have to see to all our needs ourselves, won't we?"

43

"Yes, dear," Wildon said with forced cheerfulness. "But I promise we shall engage a maid as quickly as it is possible to do so."

"Wildon, I cannot cook," Hester pointed out.

"Oh, I'm sure you can manage," Wildon said.

Ethel sucked in her breath, then cleared the table. After being instructed that a washbasin was beside the water barrel, she tended to cleaning the dishes. An hour later, she and Albert took their leave and went back to their tent.

Wildon and Hester settled down in the living room. "So how are your parents?" he asked. "And dear Fionna and Penelope?"

Hester burst into tears again.

The evening was a strained affair filled with disjointed conversation and weeping. When it was time to retire for the night, they went into the bedroom. After changing into their nightclothes, Wildon tenderly embraced her.

"Hester, darling," he pleaded softly. "Please help me through this. It is as difficult for me as it is for you."

"I love you, Wildon," Hester said. "I truly do. Let's not worry ourselves. No marriage begins smoothly under any circumstances. I think that with a little effort, we can put things right." She smiled and lifted her face for a kiss. "At least a little better."

He kissed her. "I'm so happy you are here," he said.

"I want to be with you, Wildon," she said. Hester took his hand and they walked to the bed. The young wife leaned over and pulled the covers back.

Her scream was almost as loud as when she saw

the snake.

Wildon reached down and batted the scorpion off the sheets and onto the floor. Picking up a boot, he smashed the insect. "Hester, dearest—"

Mutely she turned away and spent the night dozing in one of the chairs.

CHAPTER 5

Mrs. Second Lieutenant Hester Boothe's introduction to the other wives of the regiment was not a spontaneous affair. An undertaking of such social consequence had to be done according to a ritual as demanding as a full-dress parade complete with band and honors.

The woman who took charge of this event was Mrs. Captain Elisa Armbrewster, the wife of Wildon's troop commander. Mrs. Armbrewster was a stern-faced woman in her mid-forties. The mother of four children who had grown up and fled army life, she satisfied her frustrated maternal instincts by mothering the wives of young lieutenants. Hester, being only eighteen, was junior in age to Mrs. Armbrewster's youngest. Therefore, she received a double ration of Elisa Armbrewster's attentions.

Hester was taken in tow on the second morning after her arrival at Fort MacNeil. Firmly in Elisa Armbrewster's hands, Hester was marched up to be presented to the squadron commander's wife. This was Mrs. Major Sophie Darnell.

When Hester entered the Darnell quarters, she immediately noticed they were much better than where she and Wildon lived. The lady of the house was a heavy, large-bosomed woman with gray hair and a tired expression on her face. Everything about the fifty-year-old woman spoke of fatigue. Even her subtle snobbishness had a sort of exhaustion about it as if the woman were using the last ounces of priggery left in her soul. Hester found her tiresome and offensive, but bore up under the woman's arrogance during a visit that could only be described as an interview. Before the session ended, Mrs. Darnell knew of Hester's family—particularly the Bristol Soap side of it—and the story behind the relationship between her and Wildon.

After that ordeal, Mrs. Armbrewster trotted Hester up to the most important personage on the tour. This was the First Lady of the Regiment—Mrs. Colonel Henrietta Blandenberg. She received the callers in a manner befitting a minor monarch. Condescending, haughty, and damned sure of herself, Mrs. Blandenberg conducted her own inquisition. The only difference between her and the slightly faded hauteur of Mrs. Major Darnell was that the regimental commander's wife subtly displayed her fascination with the fact that both Hester and the young Lieutenant Boothe were monied. Hester sensed a source of succor in the woman. She took advantage of it by bemoaning the fact she had no domestic help. Hester also added the information that she could not cook. Mrs. Colonel thought she could arrange for someone's maid who cooked to also prepare enough for the Boothes. After all, due to the limited shopping opportunities, everyone ate the same thing, so it wouldn't be that much trouble to prepare extra. Smiling, Henrietta Blandenberg turned to Mrs. Captain Armbrewster and instructed her to make the arrangements.

After that profitable experience, Hester and Elisa Armbrewster marched right down officers' row once more. This time it was to meet the wives of the lower-ranking company grade officers—the captains and lieutenants.

Hester looked forward to this, thinking the wives of these officers would be closer to her own age, but she was to face another disappointment. Many of these officers, especially the captains, were middle-aged. The youngest lieutenant's wife was ten years older than Hester. After that round of introductions, Hester was taken back to her own drab quarters and left there by Elisa Armbrewster who had done her duty and left some strong hints that, in spite of Colonel Mrs. Blandenberg's special interest, there would be many and varied obligations that Hester would owe her and the other wives who outranked her.

Hester, alone for the first time that morning, reflected on what she'd just experienced. The women had been in the army for many, many years. After so much time locked away in regiments at small frontier posts, they were a provincial group. She sensed that she hadn't been fully accepted into their close-knit society. Their almost universally cold acceptance and suspicious study of her during the conversations, however brief, told the young wife that she plainly had yet to pay her dues.

Hester also noted that none seemed to have much money. Their dresses were far out of date. Although this could be put down to long periods away from fashion centers, their genteel poverty was also reflected in their homes. The drapes, furnishings, dishes, and other household items were used and drab like their clothing. In her home back in New York, her family gave such clothing and property to the household staff. In fact, these ladies lived in quarters that were not as elegant as those of the Bristol servants.

Now, very displeased and lonely, Hester once again gave in to her tears. The disparity between herself and the regimental family that Wildon had thrust her into was even more apparent. She consoled herself with the thought that at least the situation of feeding themselves had been solved.

That same evening, a corporal's wife, who worked for the first squadron commander, appeared at the Boothe doorstep with a venison stew and corn bread. The woman seemed pleased with the opportunity to make a few extra dollars each month, and Hester was very happy to pay whatever was asked.

A week later Albert and Ethel, their relief and joy visible, were put aboard the stagecoach that would carry them to the nearest railhead for the return to New York. With them gone, Hester settled into a routine. She got up with Wildon at the ungodly hour on which the army insisted. A half-hour later Sadie Tannen, their shared domestic, showed up with a pot of coffee and hardtack biscuits. Wildon ate, then left for his day's duties. Hester retired once again to sleep until a more decent hour. She then spent the rest of the day either reading alone or in some sort of activity with the other officers' wives. If she were at someone else's quarters, she hurried home to meet Wildon when the regimental bugler sounded Retreat. Her young husband was always hungry and tired after spending the day with his troop. Sadie made yet another appearance to feed them. The evening passed with more reading and talking to Wildon until it was time to retire.

Hester thought it was a ghastly existence.

But, with the announcement of the regimental officers' ball, she brightened up. The prospect of a gala evening of dancing and socializing was just what she needed to pep up her flagging spirits. The men would don the full-dress uniforms complete with epaulets and aiguillettes, though instead of the usual plumed helmets they would sport their rakish kepis.

A large portion of the quartermaster warehouse had been set aside for the event. The officers' ladies, with enlisted men detailed for the lifting and carrying did the decorating themselves. It was at that time Hester saw a slightly different view of army life. The women cooperated among themselves in donating items for the dance. Punch bowls, ladles, decorations, cake dishes, and even silverware were taken from trunks and brought to the site of the gala event. Mrs. Colonel Blandenberg directed the activities, delegated authority, and personally checked the placement of every piece of bunting. Hester, like the other lieutenants' wives, did most of the work although there was always a soldier nearby to handle any particularly heavy task. The Mrs. Majors and Mrs. Captains generally saw to it that the Mrs. Colonel's instructions were properly carried out.

But the method seemed to work. At the end of the afternoon, the entire room was ready. After being dismissed from the detail, the women hurried back to their quarters to dress for the party.

It was difficult for Hester to prepare herself properly. The only mirror available was the hand model out of her hope chest. But with Wildon dutifully holding it, she made sure her appearance was just right.

She wore a rose satin dress with ivory-colored bows. Cut as low as propriety allowed, it was sleeveless. The skirt flowed outward from her tiny waist, cascading to the ground.

Wildon expressed it all. "Hester, you are beautiful."

Hester, smiling, returned the compliment. "And you, Lieutenant Boothe, are a most dashing officer." She walked to him and kissed his cheek. "You are even more handsome now than in your cadet uniform."

Wildon didn't notice her words. He was still mesmerized by her beauty. He ruefully wondered if Captain Armbrewster would forbid his bringing Hester to functions as he had outlawed the fancy white mess jacket.

"Are you going to stand there gawking, sir, or take me to the ball?" Hester asked with a smile.

"Why, madam! To the ball—where I shall gawk some more."

They stepped out of their quarters into the dark walkway in front of officers' row. The light was dim at that time of evening. The only illumination in the area came from lamps shining through open windows. The young couple, in the best mood they'd been in for a long time, walked arm in arm to the regimental dance.

Captain and Mrs. Armbrewster emerged from their house as Wildon and Hester walked by. Armbrewster's eyes did not waver from Hester's form. Elisa Armbrewster was visibly taken aback by Hester's appearance. She managed a cold smile, the venom dripping from her words. "Good evening. You both look charming."

"Thank you," Hester said. "You and the captain are a most handsome couple yourselves."

"Oh, we are?" Armbrewster asked with a laugh. "Well! We did our best, didn't we, Ellie?"

"Let's go," Elisa said. "We must get there before the majors or the colonel."

The foursome arrived at the same time as other company grade officers. Hester received the same unfriendly glances from their wives while the men displayed silly grins. Their remarks did not improve the women's moods.

"I say! Save a dance for me, Mrs. Boothe."

"So that's what they're wearing back East now, hey? Most charming, Mrs. Boothe."

"Now the decorations are complete, Mrs. Boothe."

Loving it all, Wildon took Hester into the room. She pointed to the table where they were to sit. "I put the place names out myself, Wildon." She pointed to the red, white, and blue bunting over one wall. "And I told the soldiers how that was to go."

"You did a wonderful job," Wildon said. "That bunting is hung much better than the others."

She poked him in the ribs. "Let's sit down."

52

Once the captains and lieutenants were situated, the regimental band—at least the part of it that was detailed to play for the dance—trooped in behind their bandmaster. They went to the raised platform put down for their benefit. Once they were ready, they poised with their instruments and waited for the man in charge to raise his baton.

The moment Colonel and Mrs. Blandenberg stepped into the room, the band struck up with the regimental song. Everyone stood up as the unit's first couple, followed now by the three majors and their wives, went to their special table at the head of the room. When they reached their seats, the band ceased playing.

Colonel Blandenberg, a portly, mustachioed old officer, stepped forward. "Good evening, ladies and gentlemen," he said. "I am pleased to welcome you to Fort MacNeil's annual military ball. We wish you all a happy evening." Those simple words officially opened the function. He turned to the bandmaster. "Sergeant Gallini, the Grand March, if you please."

Once again the regiment's official song blared out over the room. Everyone formed up, according to rank and seniority within grade, to tramp in time to the music around the room. After three circuits, the band came to a crashing finish. The people returned to their tables.

Hester, glad the opening ceremonies were over, smiled when the first tune, "The Blue Danube," began to play. She looked over at Wildon.

He correctly responded. "Shall we waltz?"

"Yes, let's."

They swung around the floor with the other

53

couples. Although the music was not up to par in Hester's estimate, it was good enough to carry her into a light mood. She felt as if she were floating in Wildon's arms as they dipped and circled.

Wildon, on the other hand, noticed the looks that the other wives were continuing to give Hester. Her attire did more than enhance her own attractiveness. It contrasted so sharply with theirs that the drab, sometimes mended, out-of-date dresses they wore were revealed in their true condition. Wildon realized that if it hadn't been for Hester, it would have been just another regimental ball. But it was already ruined for many of the women. He vaguely wondered if he—and Hester—would pay a price for the unintentional rebuff.

After a couple of dances, Captain Armbrewster appeared at their table. "Hello, Mister Boothe. Might I have permission to dance with your lady?"

"Only if I may dance with yours, sir," Wildon replied.

"Of course. Mrs. Boothe?"

"My pleasure, Captain Armbrewster."

They went out on the floor and waited a moment for the band to begin. When it did, Armbrewster took her in his arms and stepped out. He was remarkably light on his feet. Armbrewster smiled. "So how do you find Fort MacNeil, Mrs. Boothe?"

"Quite nice, thank you," Hester said.

He nodded. "Your husband is a fine young officer."

"Thank you."

They completed the fox trot, then Hester was taken back to her table. A bow from the captain and he left. But Major Darnell took his place. Hester suppressed a smile as she thought of how Wildon would have to go dance with Sophie Darnell.

Once out on the dance floor, the major whirled her about. "How do you find Fort MacNeil, Mrs. Boothe?"

"Quite nice, thank you," Hester said.

"Your husband is a fine young officer. He should go far in the army."

After that dance she endured one with another major, then Colonel Blandenberg himself appeared at the table. It was another dance, same conversation, same replies, before she was delivered once again to the table. The next man to present himself was the regimental surgeon. Wildon introduced him. "Hester, this is Doctor Dempster."

"How'd you do, ma'am," he said a bit slurred. He winked at Wildon. "May I have the pleasure of dancing with your lady, old man?" He laughed. "Aren't you glad I'm a bachelor and don't have a worn hag to foist on you?"

Wildon grinned back. "Yes. Most definitely."

When Hester danced with the doctor, she found him a bit awkward. He was obviously drunk and his rhythm was off. He slightly pulled and pushed at her a few times, but at least didn't step on her feet. When he brought her back to Wildon, he affected a little bow by dipping his head in one quick movement. "Most o' the time that I dance, Mrs. Boothe, I do it out of social and milit'ry obligation. But with you, madam, I danced with pleasure. G'd evenin'."

Hester watched him walk away. "In a way, he's the most charming man I've danced with all evening."

"Hey!" Wildon said. "What about me?"

"Let me think about that," Hester said with a mischievous smile.

Wildon started to protest, but everyone's attention was attracted to the door when a sergeant appeared. He went directly to the colonel and spoke a few words to him. The colonel immediately got to his feet and followed the N.C.O. out of the building.

"Who was that?" Hester asked.

"That's Flanagan, a signal corps sergeant," Wildon explained. "He's in charge of the telegraph."

The band played two more dances. Hester was glad to be with Wildon again. Somehow the music and moving with him was relaxing. Her dark mood was lifted away, and for the first time since her arrival, she was actually glad to be where she was.

The colonel came back in and interrupted the following dance. "Ladies and gentlemen!" he said. "I have an important announcement."

Everyone, knowing how easy it was for the staid tedium of army routine to be brought suddenly to a crashing halt, gave the colonel his or her full attention.

"Orders have just been telegraphed to us," Colonel Blandenberg said. "As you know, there has been very little activity in this vicinity by hostile Indians. We have been pretty much taking our ease. Therefore, a telegram from department headquarters has arrived this evening ordering the regiment to be transferred to Fort Mojave in Arizona Territory. We are to begin the move as soon as practicable."

Hester turned and looked up at Wildon. "Thank the Lord!" she exclaimed under her breath. "At last we shall leave this horrid place."

"Yes. It appears so," Wildon replied.

"Do you know what the new fort is like?" Hester asked.

"I've heard of it," Wildon admitted. "Oh, the band is going to play again. Shall we continue the dance?"

"No! I don't like your answer to my question, Wildon," Hester said. "It was not complete. What is that place like?"

"I think," Wildon said artfully, "that it is more rustic than this one."

Hester, allowing herself to be led into a waltz, bit her lip.

CHAPTER 6

Second Lieutenant Boothe tipped back the brim of his hat. The sun, though not yet a deep orange color, was sinking toward the western horizon of the bleak, empty landscape. He looked back at the train of six baggage wagons and the regimental ambulance behind him. There were four troopers on each side of the slow convoy and two more to the rear. Up at the front, where Wildon rode, there was just himself and his second-in-command, Sgt. James Garrity.

Garrity, a muscular, grizzled man with a short-cropped gray beard, was a veteran sergeant with a quarter of a century in the U.S. Army. He had been three years into his first five-year hitch when the War between the States broke out. That was in this same cavalry regiment in which he still served. Others who now had assignments in the unit had also been with him. The present commander Colonel Blandenberg had led the third squadron as a senior captain. Major Darnell and Captain Armbrewster were both fresh-faced lieutenants in those days. They would learn some hard lessons in the four years of warfare ahead of them. When Lee surrendered at Appomattox, no peace awaited them or the regiment. Rather

58

than being posted to a cushy garrison or assigned as occupation troops in the South, the unit was sent West to fight the fierce Kiowas and Comanches in Texas.

Only recently, with the shifting of hostilities farther north, had Garrity and the others finally been able to enjoy some quiet boredom in the garrison. Now, with this latest transfer to Arizona where unbridled Apache resisted civilization's encroachment, it appeared that active fighting was once again to be a part of their lives—and deaths.

"How far do you figure we've traveled today, Sergeant?" Wildon asked.

"I'd say about fifteen miles, sir," Garrity answered.

Wildon raised his eyebrows in surprise. He'd calculated the distance himself using the mathematical skills picked up with his engineering training at West Point. His own estimate was 14.875 miles. "How did you arrive at that answer?"

Garrity shrugged and grinned with quiet humor. "I just feel about fifteen miles tired in these old soljer's bones, sir."

"My shavetail bones agree," Wildon said. He liked having the sergeant by his side. The N.C.O.'s appearance and conduct epitomized everything Wildon thought a professional soldier should be. "Let's call a halt and settle in for the night."

"Yes, sir." Garrity swung his horse around and signaled the lead wagon. The driver pulled on the reins to lead the others into a tight circle.

After two days of travel with the sergeant, Wildon knew enough to leave the organization of the camp to him. He rode back down the line of wagons until he reached the one he and Hester used as their traveling quarters. The soldier-driver saluted him from the seat. "Good evening, sir."

"Good evening, O'Leary," Wildon said.

Hester, sitting beside the teamster, looked at her husband from the shadow of the sunbonnet she wore. It was part of an outfit that had been a last-minute purchase from the sutler. Her dress was gray calico with long sleeves and a high neck. Although the attire was far from attractive, it was practical and comfortable for the long weeks of travel they faced.

O'Leary stepped down from the wagon, then turned to help Hester to the ground. After a polite tipping of his hat, the soldier set about uncoupling the pair of mules and leading them over to the animal picket line being set up under the supervision of a bad-tempered corporal.

"How did the afternoon go, dear?" Wildon asked, unhooking the tailgate.

"Lovely," Hester said in a flat voice.

Wildon hopped up into the back of the wagon and lowered two chairs to the ground. "I'll bet it was dusty at times," he said cheerfully.

"It was dusty *all* the time," Hester said, sitting down.

Their conversation was interrupted by Surgeon Schuyler Dempster walking by. "Good evening, folks," he said cheerfully. "How was the ride today?"

Hester didn't bother to answer.

"Oh, well," Dempster said, sensing her displeasure, "a few more weeks and this will all be over. I shall see you later." He tipped his hat and walked toward the other side of the wagons.

Wildon reached into the wagon and pulled out their cooking pots. "Well, I'll have a fire going and we'll enjoy some nice hot coffee. How does that sound?"

"Wonderful."

Quartermaster Sergeant Mulvaney appeared at the Boothe wagon. As the commanding officer, Wildon received constant callers. "Good evening, sir. Top o' the day, Mrs. Boothe."

"Yes, Sergeant Mulvaney?" Wildon asked.

"Sir, I'm happy to report that there's no problems with wagons or animals," Mulvaney said. "I've checked the convoy and ever'thing is standing tall."

"That's fine," Wildon said, glad to have some good news. "I presume the problem with the wheel on the water wagon has been taken care of."

"Indeed it has, sir," Mulvaney said. "We greased her up and tightened her down. She'll last to Fort Mojave."

"Good evening, folks." Mulvaney's wife Dixie joined them, carrying a steaming pot.

Hester sighed at this latest interruption, but kept her irritation to herself. "How do you do."

Dixie was a short, stocky woman with faded red hair and a good-humored face covered with freckles. "I've a bit of extra p'tato soup and I thought it might go well here."

"Indeed, Mrs. Mulvaney!" Wildon exclaimed. He had not been eating well at all. Hester's attempts at cooking amounted to only boiled salt pork and hardtack soaked in coffee. "It is most appreciated, thank you so much."

Hester, smiling slightly, continued to sit in the

chair.

Dixie, waiting for a few moments, finally spoke to her. "If you had some bowls, I could ladle you out a bit."

Hester finally took the hint and got up to fetch a couple of bowls stowed in the rear of the wagon. She held them out while Dixie gave them a generous helping of her soup. "There's a bit o' peas and carrots in there too."

"It smells delicious," Wildon said. "We've not been enjoying very fancy cuisine on this trip."

"Well now," Dixie said diplomatically. "If you could use some help or would like me to share a recipe, just say the word."

Mulvaney laughed. "My darling Dixie has cooked under far worse conditions that this. And she knows how to fill a family's bellies, believe me."

"Thank you," Hester said coldly. "I shall keep your kind offer in mind."

"By your leave, sir," Mulvaney said, saluting. "I'll get back to me own wagon for a hot supper."

"We'll be seeing you," Dixie said.

After the Mulvaneys made their exit, Wildon and Hester gave their full attention to the delicious soup. Hester consumed her meal slowly, her eyes gazing out past the wagons to the desolate desert area. "What is it you said they call this place, Wildon?"

"The Llano Estacado," he answered. "That means the Staked Plain in Spanish. I read up a bit on it. It's approximately thirty thousand square miles of semi-arid plain. Not much water and a high evaporation rate, so any rainfall doesn't stick around much."

"It that why we must carry our water with us?"

Hester asked.

"Yes," Wildon said. "You can find some out here now and then, but I'm afraid it's not too tasty."

"I suppose washing is out of the question, isn't it?" Hester asked.

"I'm afraid so, darling. But bear up," he said. "It's only a temporary thing."

"God in heaven, Wildon!" she exclaimed. "This dreary trip is going to take three or four weeks." The journey had been an emotional slap in the face to the young woman. Not only could she not wash, but tending to nature's call was done in the open. Then women went to the left of the train and the men to the right. Hester found squatting down and relieving herself behind the dubious privacy afforded by withered desert plants an embarrassment. The other women, all enlisted men's wives, chatted gaily among themselves during these times. Hester withdrew from them as much as possible. She found their company disagreeable under any circumstances, but particularly trying in the present lack of decorum.

Wildon stopped eating. "I'm terribly sorry, darling. I truly am."

Hester took another bite of her soup. "I do not know why you have chosen this awful life. Haven't you considered the choices available to us back in New York? If you don't care for your own family's business, perhaps you would accept a position in mine. Father could find you any number of interesting and well-paying positions."

"I've always wanted to be a soldier," Wildon said almost defensively.

"Then why not be one back in the East?" Hester

63

asked. "Your own uncle could see that you would be stationed at some nice fort in New England."

"Darling, I chose the cavalry as my branch because I knew the chances for active service in the Indian wars were the greatest," Wildon said. "I thought it rather nice if I could become a general someday. I could never attain high rank going through useless parades at some fancy-pants post. That is why I want active campaigning."

Hester set her bowl on the ground. "I guess I'm not very hungry this evening."

He finished his soup. "I must find Sergeant Garrity and inspect the guard. I'll be back in a half-hour or so."

"Take your time."

Wildon stood up and started to say something. Changing his mind, he walked across the inner area of the circled wagons to the soldiers' area. His mind felt crushed by the realization of the inevitable clash building up in his marriage.

The regiment's physical transfer to Fort Mojave, Arizona Territory, had been a carefully planned military operation. Colonel Blandenberg sat down with his squadron commanders, adjutant, quartermaster, and staff noncommissioned officers to put everything down on paper. The actual route to follow across New Mexico was minutely traced on maps with special consideration being given to the wagons and the families of the men.

An advance party, made up of unmarried officers and soldiers, would go ahead in order to arrive at the new post and begin the preliminary preparations for the arrival of the main body. The bulk of the regiment would follow them in twenty-four hours. A third element, one day behind them, would be a wagon train made up of nonessential baggage supervised and cared for by the quartermaster sergeant. This group would also make a last-minute inspection of Fort MacNeil to make sure it had been properly cleared and that no U.S. property had been inadvertently left behind.

Since no hostile Indians were in the area, only a small escort of troops would be required. This insignificant duty was assigned to the most junior officer—2d Lt. Wildon Boothe—to command. Sergeant Garrity was assigned to help him with the ten men in the detachment. Quartermaster Sergeant Mulvaney would be in charge of the teamsters. Colonel Blandenberg also was considerate enough to allow not only Lieutenant Boothe's wife to accompany him, but also three other women married to soldiers in the group.

The final addition to the little wagon train was Surgeon Schuyler Dempster and his hospital orderly. They and their baggage would travel in the ambulance.

Since no potable water would be available in rivers and creeks, a water wagon was made available in each of the three groups. Government rations, consisting of salt pork and hardtack, would also be the bare minimum. If any of the married couples were willing to carry their own food, they were free to eat as they pleased, keeping in mind that firewood would be scarce.

It was under these conditions that Wildon and Hester took up temporary residence in the back of a government-issue wagon. All their furniture, bedding, clothing, and other belongings were piled in. Wildon spent the day leading the little baggage train across the expanse of the Llano Estacado while his wife sat on the hard, bouncing seat of the wagon beside an army teamster.

She could have borne up under the strain if they had been headed for a nice post. But putting up with the present physical hardship to go to a worse place made the very idea of the journey an abomination.

The clear persistent notes of Reveille sounded over the camp. Wildon, responding with the same instinctive fervor he had done at West Point, sat straight up before he was fully awake. In doing so, he dragged the covers off Hester. She moaned loudly and woke up as the cold air swept over her.

"Wildon!" she hissed angrily, grabbing the blankets.

"We have to get up, dear," Wildon said. He crawled over to where his uniform was piled and quickly dressed in the dark. "I must see that the men are ready to move out as soon as possible."

"Can't that Sergeant Garrity take care of that?"

"He will, dear," Wildon explained. "But I must be there to take his report."

Hester, silently damning the United States Cavalry to an eternity in hell, struggled into the awful dress that circumstances now forced her to wear. She'd just slipped into her shoes when the driver could be heard outside the wagon bringing up the mule team.

"Mrs. Boothe!" The shrill voice of Dixie Mulvaney sounded over the tailgate. "Mrs. Boothe!"

Hester gritted her teeth. "Yes?"

The woman's face, lit by a nearby flickering campfire, appeared at the rear of the vehicle. "Good morning, Mrs. Boothe. I brung you and the lieutenant some hot coffee."

"Thank you," Hester said. She could smell the brew, and it was a welcome aroma in spite of her dislike for Dixie. Bent double, she walked toward the rear of the wagon. It was jostled by the soldier hitching up the mules to it and she stumbled.

Dixie laughed. "Now ain't this a hell of a life?"

"Yes, Mrs. Mulvaney," Hester said grimly as she slipped down to the ground. "This is, indeed, a hell of a life." She took the tin cup and treated herself to a sip. "Thank you very much."

"Sure now and you're welcome," Dixie said. "It's hard to get up now and then, ain't it?"

"It is difficult any time," Hester said.

"I'd be happy to wake you a bit early," Dixie offered. "That way you could have some coffee ready for the lieutenant before he went to his duties."

Hester didn't like that idea one bit. "No, thank you."

"It's no trouble a'tall," Dixie assured her. "After twenty years as an army wife, I sleep with one eye open anyway."

"I intend to sleep with both my eyes firmly shut," Hester said angrily. "And as far as Wildon having a hot cup of coffee in the morning. I couldn't care less."

Dixie smiled. The sergeant's wife was not a stupid woman. She had sensed Hester's dislike for her, but put it down to being new, confused, and unhappy. "It's terrible difficult the first few years, my dear, but—"

"I'll not be here twenty years, Mrs. Mulvaney," Hester interrupted. She greedily drank down the coffee and handed the cup back. "Will you excuse me, please?"

"Of course, ma'am."

Hester walked away from the camp and out into the desert. After going fifty yards she found a knee-high scrub. Looking around, she pulled down her drawers and lifted her skirt. Squatting there, she relieved herself, thinking of the fine water closet back at her home on Lake Champlain's shore.

"God!" she thought. "If Penelope and Fionna could only see me now!"

After finishing, she straightened her clothes and walked back. The team was hitched up and the driver waiting. Her face crimsoned with the thought he knew what she'd been doing. But the soldier seemed unaffected. "Good morning, Mrs. Boothe. Are you ready to hop up on the seat?"

"Yes. Thank you," Hester said. She allowed the man to help her up onto the high seat.

Wildon rode up, reining in beside her. "I just got a cup of coffee from Mrs. Mulvaney. She says she'd visited you already."

"Yes," Hester said.

"Nice lady," Wildon said. "It's time to move out. I shall see you later, dear."

Surgeon Dempster appeared on his way to his own

vehicle. "A good morning to you, Mrs. Boothe. It appears you're all set for another day of travel, hey?" He walked on by without waiting for a reply.

It was just as well. Hester didn't feel like talking. She braced herself for another jolting, miserable day on the wagon seat.

CHAPTER 7

The afternoon seemed an endless, hot ordeal. The men slumped in their saddles while the teamsters let the natural movement of the plodding mules pull the wagons with a minimum of physical or vocal guidance.

Even Wildon, usually enthusiastic and energetic about any aspect of military life, dozed from time to time. He fought the sleepiness in various ways. Wishing there was enough water so he could enjoy the luxury of splashing some onto his face, he stood in the stirrups, dismounted for walks beside his mount, and even slapped himself once or twice. But he still occasionally dozed off.

Each time he snapped back awake, he would look sheepishly over at Sergeant Garrity. The N.C.O. was always wide awake and unaffected by the lethargy that blanketed the baggage train.

Finally, in spite of all his efforts, the young second lieutenant sank into a deep sleep, instinctively maintaining his seat on the horse's back. The plop-plop sound of the hooves on the hard sand seemed almost hypnotic. He dreamed a bit about himself and Hester back in New York. Like all mental images conjured up in slumber, this one was disjointed and unreal. People he knew at Fort MacNeil were there at Lake Champlain. But suddenly there was a disturbance in his napping. The clopping of the horse was now interspersed by loud popping sounds that quickly grew in intensity.

"Flankers in!" Sergeant Garrity bellowed. "Circle the wagons! Move, goddamn you, move!"

Wildon's eyes popped open. He looked around and saw riders making a wide circuit around the wagon train as the mule-drawn vehicles slowly turned into a defensive formation. Then it dawned on him that the horsemen were shooting at them.

"Indians?"

"No, sir," Garrity answered. "Border raiders."

Another look by Wildon confirmed that he and his group were indeed under fire. Although the shooting was inaccurate because of the range and the fact the assault was being conducted on horseback, the situation was still dangerous. The officer studied the unexpected adversaries. They seemed a diverse group. Some were dressed as Mexicans with wide sombreros. Others had the appearance of being American cowboys. A good number wore combinations of not only those two modes of dress but affected certain articles of Indian costumes too.

Wildon's first instinct was to rush back to stick close to Hester, but as the commanding officer he had duties that prevented him from following his marital desires as a husband and protector. He noted that the flankers and rear guard had now moved in close and were returning fire at the bandits who were keeping their distance.

"Sergeant Garrity!" he shouted. "Take command of the right section!"

"Yes, sir!"

Wildon galloped into the wagons. "Dismount," he ordered the cavalrymen. "Find cover among the wagons. You teamsters! Get down from those seats."

"Wildon!" Hester's voice sounded over the shooting.

He slid from the saddle, taking a final look to make sure he was being obeyed. Then he rushed to his wife. "Hurry down, darling."

"Wildon, please tell me what is happening," Hester said irritably as she allowed him to help her from the wagon seat. "What is all this shooting about?"

"Bandits, my dear," Wildon said. "Don't worry, but please stay down."

Hester obeyed, wincing at the noise of nearby soldiers firing their weapons. Dixie Mulvaney scurried up and took her hand. "Stay low now, Mrs. Boothe. I've a lovely trunk me darling husband just tumbled to the ground. We can squat safe and cozy behind that."

"No, thank you," Hester said irritably.

But Wildon spoke up sharply. "Go with her," Wildon said flatly and with authority in his voice.

Hester had never seen or heard her husband in such a determined or serious mood. She knew it was time for obedience, not discussion. "Yes, darling." She allowed herself to be led away by Dixie.

Wildon watched them go, breathing easier when he saw them reach the safety near the Mulvaney wagon.

By then Sergeant Garrity and his section were in

position. The tightness of the wagons' circle brought the small command into one group. Wildon took overall command, but sought out the N.C.O.

"Who are those men?" he asked.

"A border gang, sir," Garrity explained. "There's a lot of such riffraff in this part of the country. Most of 'em are the worst kind of desperado."

The bandits continued their wide circle, firing ineffectually. The soldiers and teamsters were armed with Model 1872 Springfield carbines. The breechloaded weapons fired a .45-caliber bullet. All veterans of Indian warfare, the troopers carefully aimed each shot, squeezing off their rounds in deliberate fashion as they coolly returned fire.

But Wildon, an expert hunter, was not very impressed with their marksmanship.

"Give them some lead. You're shooting behind them!" he yelled. Finally, in exasperation, he went up to one of the soldiers and took his carbine. He sighted on a bandit with a large yellow sombrero and striped serape. Instinctively judging the distance, Wildon moved the sights to adjust for the windage. He pulled the trigger and saw the man's arms fly up as he tumbled over the rump of his horse.

The men cheered. "Nice shot, Lieutenant!"

"Good on you, Mister Boothe!"

Wildon grinned and handed the carbine back. He turned to retrace his steps, then froze.

"Oh, my God!"

The full realization that he had just shot a man—a human being—and probably killed him hit him hard and fully. He swallowed hard and his face blanched.

Garrity, standing nearby, noticed the effect. He

walked up to the young lieutenant. "Now you've done it."

"Huh?"

"It was gonna happen sometime, sir," Garrity said. "You don't soldier without killing somebody."

"God!" Wildon said. "My baptism of fire." He took a deep breath.

"You'll be all right, sir," Garrity assured him. "There's not a man jack here that ain't been through it."

The awful feeling quickly subsided. Wildon knew why. "There is a bit of a difference in this situation that sets me aside from the ordinary, Sergeant. My wife happens to be here in this my first battle."

"Yes, sir," Garrity said. "You're protecting her from those animals out there. And that's exactly what the bastards are. Merciless, cruel devils. They're worse than Injuns, sir."

Wildon went back to the line of wagons and took another man's carbine. After a couple of shots he returned to Garrity. "I think I'm back to being able to think clearly and coolly."

"Yes, sir," Garrity agreed.

Wildon studied the desperados for a few moments as the sporadic shooting continued. "What the hell do they think they're doing?" he asked Garrity. "There's not enough of them to pose a really serious threat."

The sergeant shook his head. "Hard to tell. They're keeping their distance. Could be that the sonofabitches think they can wear us down."

"I would say a vigorous charge would break their line and force them into a retreat, Sergeant," Wildon said.

"I don't know, sir," Garrity said. "There might be more of 'em on the way. Or maybe just waiting out there for us to ride into an ambush."

"Well, I do," Wildon said. "Mount the two sections and we'll drive the scoundrels off and continue our trip."

"I wish you'd wait a bit, Lieutenant," Garrity said. "We really don't know the situation yet."

Wildon, not much giving to swearing in the past, decided it was time. "By hell's fires," he swore awkwardly. "I say we form up and charge the damned bastards, Sergeant. Form the men."

Garrity saluted. "Sections fall in to horse!" he shouted. "One rank!"

The men, sensing something was about to happen, quickly obeyed.

"Prepare to mount—*mount!*" Garrity yelled.

The ten men swung up on their horses' backs. Wildon got into his own saddle and rode to the front. "Draw pistols! Forward at a walk, *yo!*"

The two sections rode slowly through the circle of wagons until they were out in the open.

"Forward at a gallop, *yo!*" Wildon commanded. "Raise pistols!"

Now, moving faster with their pistols held high, the troopers' excitement grew with the prospect of combat.

"Charge!"

Now, cheering wildly, they broke into a full charge. The horses, caught up in the frenzy of the moment like their riders, eagerly bounded forward, picking up speed with each stride.

The bandits, seeing the sight of twelve, fully armed cavalry troopers racing toward them, broke their circle. They turned toward the south and began a wild rout away from the scene of the initial battle.

Wildon, grinning in vicious happiness, urged his horse on. He tried to take aim with his pistol, but couldn't get a good sight to draw. He contented himself with wild shots at the group of desperados.

The chase veered off to the left, then swung slightly around as the two groups of riders headed for some low foothills. Several times the *bandidos* were momentarily hidden from view as they rode down the far side of a rise, popping up to disappear down the next incline.

But the final time, they did not reappear.

Garrity forced his own mount to increase its speed until he caught up with the lieutenant. "Sir!" he bellowed in alarm. "Turn about for Christ's sake! Turn about!"

Wildon, angry and puzzled, started to reply, but his words were cut off by a roaring fusillade to the front. He whipped his eyes back in that direction and saw twice as many bandits as before—and they were galloping straight back at them.

Bullets, flying close by, zapped through the air or slapped into the ground, kicking up large spurts of dirt. It was not necessary to issue any orders. All the soldiers pulled hard on their reins and turned their horses back in the opposite direction. Now, riding frantically, the pursuers had become the pursued.

The same terrain was traveled in the flight back to the wagon train. Wildon, fully knowing his duties as an officer, kept his horse from overtaking those of his soldiers. It was utter stupidity to try to shoot back at the desperados chasing them, so the cavalry troops concentrated on one of the oldest maneuvers in military history—getting the hell out of a dangerous situation.

Finally they crested the last hill before the rush down to the wagons. The thrilling joy of reaching safety was suddenly dashed. Several of the wagons were burning, and Wildon could see a couple of teamsters sprawled out on the ground. Wildon glanced back and now noted that the outlaws chasing them had turned and galloped off. Turning his full attention back to reaching the vehicles, he passed the men as he raced the remainder of the way across the sand.

Quartermaster Sergeant Mulvaney, pistol in hand, was waiting for him. He quickly saluted and reported. "Sir, more of 'em hit us after you left. They came in hard and fast and took one side of the formation."

Wildon glanced wildly around for Hester. "Yes! Yes, Sergeant Mulvaney. Go on."

"They took a look in the wagons and figgered we didn't have nothing worth looting and took off," Mulvaney said. "Then you showed up."

Dixie Mulvaney, disheveled and excited, rushed up to them, shouting, "They took your missus, Lieutenant Boothe!"

Wildon's eyes opened wide. "What?" The words seemed so absurd as to not make sense. "What did you say?"

"One of them heathen devils grabbed her up," Dixie said, gasping. "He rode off with her across his saddle."

"Goddamn it!" Wildon said, now swearing fluently. "Sergeant Garrity! Mount the sections!"

"Hold it, sir," Garrity said. "The same thing would happen again. We'd get ambushed for sure."

"I'm not letting them ride off with my wife!" Wildon shouted. "Are you crazy? What the hell do you think I'm going to do?"

"He's right, sir," Mulvaney said. "You've got to think this through."

"There is nothing to think about!" the distraught young husband shouted wildly. "Goddamn your eyes, Garrity! I gave an order! Mount those sections!"

"Sir, listen," Garrity said. "A detachment can't get her back."

Wildon could barely control himself. "Then I'll—"

"Listen, Lieutenant!" Garrity shouted. He did not wish to be insubordinate, but it was the only way to get the distraught young man's full attention. When Wildon finally exhibited an indication to listen, the sergeant continued. "Sir, two men could track them down and find her."

The cool logic behind the words broke through Wildon's hysteria. "Yes! Yes!" He took a deep breath. "What do you suggest, Sergeant?"

"You and me, sir," Garrity said. "We can get out of uniform and into our civilian gear."

"What the hell for? It's a waste of time," Wildon insisted in his returning excitement.

"Sir, we ain't gonna ride out there and pull her away. We'll have to spend some time scouting and trailing. It will help us to be in civilian clothes."

"I have a buckskin outfit," Wildon said. "I use it for hunting."

"I know, sir," Garrity said, relieved to see Wildon was coming under control. "That's a fine idea. I have a buckskin jacket myself. I can wear that and my other duds. We'll look like a coupla drifters. That way we can poke around and find your wife."

"Right. Then we can rush them and rescue Hester," Wildon said.

"Let's find her first, sir," Garrity said. "Then we'll figger out a course to take. Please get changed."

Mulvaney nodded his agreement. "I'll take the wagon train on meself, sir. You can catch up with us later."

Wordlessly, Wildon sprang into action. He turned and rushed toward his wagon to follow Sergeant Garrity's instructions.

"Oh, God!" Dixie wailed. "They'll never—"

"Hush, woman!" Mulvaney said.

Dixie started to weep. "That poor, poor girl."

CHAPTER 8

Hester sat on the horse with her hands tied in front of her. She grasped the saddle horn as best she could while maintaining her balance on the galloping animal. A man rode to her direct front, holding the reins of her mount in his right fist as he controlled the stallion he rode with his left. He glanced back at her many times, smiling at the young woman in a way that she did not sense as hostile or threatening. But his gaze still unnerved her.

Hester, dazed by what had happened an hour previously, finally began to think straight. She had been dozing on the wagon seat, leaning back against the front hoop, when the shooting broke out. The teamsters had immediately obeyed orders by following the other vehicles into a circle. Unsure and curious about what was going on, she watched as some strange men galloped around the baggage train shooting at it. Finally Wildon arrived and made her get down to join Dixie Mulvaney behind her trunk.

Dixie had been frightened, but angrily defiant too.

She'd mumbled confusing things to Hester, talking about how they should shoot themselves if the bandits killed all the men. Then she'd cheered and said how all the bandits in the world couldn't defeat the United States Cavalry. But her mood had turned dark again, and she spoke rapidly of dying rather than allowing herself to become a prisoner of the raiders.

Hester, although prepared by her mother for her wedding night, was still inexperienced and too sheltered to completely comprehend the reason behind Dixie Mulvaney's irrational behavior.

Finally Wildon and the others mounted up and drove off the attackers. A cheer came from Sergeant Mulvaney and the teamsters, but their joy did not last long. A larger group of attackers swept down on them and rushed into the group of wagons. From that point on, events turned into a tumble of confusing images. Hester remembered seeing two of the teamsters mysteriously collapse to the ground, then suddenly she was swept up off her feet and flung across a saddle.

After a wild painful ride, her abductor came to a halt. Hester saw him clearly for the first time. He was a thin, hawk-nosed man with a waxed mustache. Although he was rough looking in his bandit attire, his eyes showed a degree of intelligence, and his manners were somewhat refined in spite of the violent way in which he held her across his saddle.

She realized he was the leader when some of the other raiders suddenly showed up. He spoke to them in a foreign language and they produced a horse. After tying Hester's hands, they placed her aboard the animal and they rode off.

Now, with her head clearing, Hester finally gave serious thought to the fact she must escape. Suddenly she reached forward and grabbed the horse's bridle. With a quick pull, she turned the animal, freeing its reins from the grasp of the man in front of her. Hester kicked her heels into the mount's flank and it responded rapidly. She could hear the wild cheers of the bandits as she streaked for freedom.

An expert rider, Hester had no trouble keeping her seat in the saddle while pulling the reins up even with her hands tied together. Once she had the leather straps in her grasp, she was better able to control the horse. The wind whipped her hair in the wild ride. But she noticed the men coming up alongside her. The horse she was on was not the swiftest of the group. She swung the animal to the right, then cut back to the left. The maneuver gained her some ground.

Now the pursuers were so close that the sound of their horses' hooves blended in with those of the one she rode. A pounding, thundering roar engulfed the scene as the young woman desperately urged the spirited animal to greater effort.

But it was no use.

The thin man came up alongside her, reached over and grasped the bridle. Hester wished she had a riding crop with which to strike him. Finally he slowed her down enough to gain complete control, and they stopped.

"Let me go!" Hester cried out.

The man laughed. "A woman with spirit! Ah! And such beauty too!" He spoke with a heavy accent.

"My husband is an officer in the United States Army," Hester said. "He'll get you for this."

"How bad for me," the man said. He stood up in the stirrups and affected a bow as he doffed his sombrero. "Allow me to introduce myself, please, most beautiful American lady. I am Hubert Mauveaux."

"I demand that you release me!"

"Ah! You will not tell me who you are?" Mauveaux said. "Then how are we to speak one to the other, eh?"

Hester hesitated, then said, "I am Mrs. Wildon Boothe. My husband is Lieutenant Wildon Boothe. Now, sir, I will thank you to allow me to return to my husband and friends."

"Alas, impossible!" Mauveaux said. "I am smitten with you."

Hester's temper snapped. "You brute!" She attempted to ride away, but he held on tightly to the bridle. Infuriated, she struck him with her bound hands. "Unhand that horse, sir!"

"I must tell you, Mrs. Wildon Boothe, that you are going to go with me," Mauveaux said. "I insist on it." He turned to one of the bandits standing nearby. *Dame una reata pronto!*

The man pulled his lariat from his saddle and tossed it over. Mauveaux caught it and dismounted. He firmly grasped Hester's leg. "Forgive, please, my familiarity," he said. "I only do it out of necessity." He could see the shape of her calf under the thin calico skirt. "Such loveliness!" He tied it tight to the stirrup strap. Then he slipped under her horse, taking the loose end of the rope with him. He used it to secure her other leg. "Forgive my barbarism," Mauveaux said, getting back on his own mount. "But you have made it the necessity, no?"

"Sir, I protest!" Hester said in a firm voice.

"Of course you do," Mauveaux replied, smiling. "But I also must make a protest, for you are breaking my heart."

"If my husband gets his hands on you, he'll break more than your heart, sir!" Hester snapped. She found the man to be extremely strange. He kept and treated her as a prisoner, yet he kept intoning romantic phrases. She didn't quite know how to judge her circumstances. "I warn you! I shall get away from you, sir!"

"Ah! The pursuit!" Mauveaux exclaimed. "It is like the appetizer before the feast—tantalizing, promising, and an exciting hint of the tastes to follow." He turned to his men and signaled. *Ya, vamanos a la montaña.*

Hester, firmly tied in place, had no choice but to allow herself to be led away by Mauveaux the bandit chief.

Hubert Mauveaux had been born into a wealthy family in Orleans, France. His father was an art dealer who spent a great deal of time away from home on buying trips. The mother, a beautiful but slightly dull-witted woman, was years younger than her drudge of a husband. Rather than pine away in boredom in her dull marriage, the young wife amused herself with countless love affairs, contenting herself with turning over the actual raising of her son to a succession of nannies.

As a toddler, Mauveaux had been prone to violent temper tantrums that would turn his face purple from the screaming and exertion of the fits. As a young child, a streak became apparent in his make-up of treating his pets cruelly that shocked and dismayed the household staff. Later, as he grew older, he vented these sadistic displays toward smaller children.

However, when he reached his teens, a tender side to Mauveaux' emotional make-up became evident. He evolved into an incurable romantic, with mad infatuations directed toward any female, receptive or not, who caught his fancy. The drawback to these amorous tendencies was that he could not take no for an answer. This led to more complications when his brutality, fed by the frustration of refusal, overrode his affections for the female concerned.

His amorous attentions were directed toward women as diverse as serving wenches in cheap bistros to young women of his own class. He courted them with flowers, poems, songs, and endless pleas for their love and devotion. Most of these episodes were harmless affairs, and the women were no more than annoyed by the gawky youngster. But when he reached his late teens, he found a special attraction to married women. When irate husbands stepped into the picture, things turned serious and ugly. At one time there were even serious possibilities of duels.

His father got Mauveaux out of those numerous scrapes. That included the several challenges of honor that had to be dealt with. With angry husbands of lesser social standing, a few thousand francs generally smoothed things over.

Finally, the older man had tried to employ his son in his art business, but Mauveaux was hopeless. Unappreciative and with no concept of value or esthetics, he bungled several big deals. That left but one solution—banish the boy to the army.

A young man from their social class could not be expected to serve as a common soldier, but it was impossible to get Mauveaux a commission in a regular regiment. Although many officers were not much more than dandies, they still had to meet certain educational qualifications. After searching around and attempting to use the influence of friends in government, Mauveaux Senior obtained a lieutenancy for Mauveaux Junior in a regiment of *chasseurs d'Afrique*. This outfit, stationed in Algeria, was a colonial unit that would never see duty in metropolitan France.

Mauveaux at first resented this posting out into what he considered a wilderness. But once he'd settled into the officers' mess and learned to find his way around, the young *sous lieutenant* was completely at home. He reveled in the North African bordellos filled with prostitutes of every nationality who would cater to any sexual desire. Between visits to the exotic whores, Mauveaux had illicit affairs with the wives of uncaring men. All the while he neglected his duties in an outrageous fashion. But nobody cared, for all an officer was expected to do was to be brave in battle.

But Mauveaux's Algerian adventures came to an

end in 1861 when his regiment was posted to Mexico to participate in Napoleon III's attempt to create a Latin League. Serving under poor deluded Emperor Maximilian and the insane Empress Carlotta, Mauveaux simply took up where he left off when he boarded the troopship in Oran.

But he discovered a new vice: gambling.

Poker became his passion, and he played the game as he had courted women—recklessly, badly, and with rotten luck. His losses mounted to such an extent that not even the allowance from his father was enough to pull him out of debt. His final fall occurred in one period of three tumultuous days when he was caught cheating at cards and stealing from his regimental officers' mess fund. Court-martialed, cashiered, and disowned by his family, Mauveaux was stuck in Mexico. He drifted into petty crime at first. When the need for money became greater, he moved to serious crime. By the time the French had been kicked out of the country, he was into banditry, using his military training to plan and lead organized raids against isolated ranches and villages. Because of his successes, he eventually built up a superb criminal organization that consisted of Americans, Mexicans, mestizos, Indians, and other half-civilized types spawned by the cruel life of the frontier. Finally in a world where his word was law, Hubert Mauveaux took whatever he wanted.

What he wanted at the particular time was Hester Boothe.

Hester, now watched more carefully, had no choice

but to cooperate as she was led up a mountainous trail. It was a narrow track with room for no more than two horses abreast. Regularly spaced guard posts were in evidence as they ascended higher into the mountains.

Mauveaux, ahead of her, looked back now and again. He winked at times. On other occasions he blew her kisses. Hester, filled with hatred and fear, did nothing to hide her distress or the revulsion she felt. These obvious signs of rejection only served to inflame the Frenchman's desires.

After an hour of slow, sure climbing, the outlaw column emerged over a crest and rode down into a wide basin. This large depression was a natural fort with immense boulders along the rim that an ancient volcano had tossed indiscriminately into position.

This was *Montaña Bandido* — Bandit Mountain — the stronghold of the Mauveaux gang. Hester sat straight and dignified as she was led across the wide expanse. She could see the hovels of the lower-ranking members of the gang. Some of these were no more than blankets thrown over a frame of limbs and lumber. Others were Apache-style wickiups, while some of the people had gone to the trouble of putting up sturdy adobe structures. But the main edifice, a two-storied building complete with a tiled roof, rose up in the center of the sprawling village.

Mauveaux pointed to it. "The people call it *El Castillo* — the Castle. It is my home, and rightfully so, for I am the king of this mountain."

Hester said nothing. She noticed that the women of the camp were gathering around, following her closely. She couldn't understand what they were saying, but it was obvious they were giving her a close scrutiny, and their voices did not sound very friendly. One in particular stared up at her with undisguised hatred. The savage look in the Latin woman's face was more frightening to the confused American girl than Mauveaux's romantic attentions.

The woman shouted to the bandit chief. *"Quien es ella?"*

Mauveaux smirked. *"No te preocupas."* He looked back at Hester and laughed. "Her name is Lola. She is terribly jealous of you."

"Please tell her she has no reason to be," Hester said.

Mauveaux laughed louder. "Yes, she does!"

"Of course she doesn't," Hester insisted.

"Already your beauty has inflamed the jealous tempers of the women," Mauveaux said in a boastful tone. "The ones who love me madly are already torn by the realization that my heart now belongs to you."

Hester almost sneered. "My husband is going to put a bullet through that heart of yours."

"To die for you, my *bellisima,* would be a most wonderful death," Mauveaux said.

When they arrived at the Castle, Mauveaux's staff was waiting. Surprisingly, they were three older women. The "king" obviously did not want romance to interfere with the efficient running of his household. He barked a few words of Spanish at them. Two of them came forward to untie Hester. The third, who seemed to be directing the other two, merely stood back and waited. Hester was pulled from the horse, then tugged toward the door. Before she entered the building, she took another desperate look around.

She now fully realized that her chances of being rescued were nil.

CHAPTER 9

Wildon urged his horse up the sharp incline from what appeared to be a dry creek bed. The animal struggled upward, then finally reached the top where Sergeant Garrity waited. The N.C.O. pointed to the south. "That's where we're headed," he said. "Mexico."

Wildon only treated the distant view to a quick glimpse. He turned his attention back to the ground. "There is still a trail evident enough to be followed."

"Yes, sir," Garrity said.

"So why are we tarrying, Sergeant?" the lieutenant demanded to know.

"We don't want to stumble into the bandits and get ourselves a big nasty surprise," Garrity explained patiently. "It will be better if we find out where they are, then make our moves, sir. That way we can decide what's going to happen — not them desperados."

"I'll trust to your caution, Sergeant," Wildon said.

"Yes, sir." Garrity pulled out a cigar and bit off the end. "There's one more thing, sir."

"What's that, Sergeant?"

"Military courtesy is going to have to cease while

we're scouting around in any towns down here. Or when we're around somebody," Garrity said. "As far as anyone is to know, we're just a couple of border drifters. If any of the bandits' agents or spies figure out we're a couple of army men from the wagon train, we'll be dead meat."

"Are you trying to tell me that a gang of cutthroats actually employs a network of organized informers, Sergeant?" Wildon asked.

"That's right, Lieutenant," Garrity explained. "These *bandido* gangs are small armies. In fact, a lot of 'em are led by former army officers who've lost out in revolutions and other power plays among the Mexican bigwigs."

"I see," Wildon said. "Then you're right, Sergeant. We had best dispense with army protocol when the situation calls for it." He smiled sheepishly. "I don't believe this ever came up in any of my West Point classes."

Garrity nodded. "Maybe you should write a lecture covering the subject, sir."

"I might at that, Sergeant. Shall we practice? I believe your first name is James, is it not, Ser — er, James?"

"Jim will do fine. Or you can call me Garrity."

"Very well, Jim. Please call me Wildon."

"Right, Wildon," Garrity said. "Let's go."

The two, as suggested by Garrity, rode with the sergeant carefully noting the trail left by the *bandidos*. Wildon gave his attention to keeping an eye on the surrounding terrain to avoid an ambush. It was the most practical arrangement since the lieutenant's education at the military academy also failed to include classes in tracking fugitives across rocky deserts.

Both men were out of uniform. Wildon was dressed in his buckskin hunting clothing complete with his privately owned Remington pistol and Winchester carbine. Garrity had borrowed the lieutenant's other long gun—a Henry repeater—but carried his army-issue Colt revolver. The pair also wore civilian belts and holsters. Their appearance was no different than a thousand other men roaming the untamed border country in the conduct of various enterprises—legal and otherwise.

Their careful tracking activities continued through the morning and into the early afternoon without stopping. At times when it was easy to determine the direction the bandits had traveled through following a logical trail, Garrity managed to save time by cutting across the circuitous route the desperados had chosen. Finally, in the early evening, Garrity halted.

"Look at this."

Wildon rode over to him. "What is it?"

"One of the horses suddenly veered off," Garrity said, pointing to the ground. "See how several others either went with it or after it?"

"Yes," Wildon said. "Perhaps an escape attempt?"

"Is Mrs. Boothe a good rider?" Garrity asked.

"She's an expert," Wildon said proudly. "She can ride as good or better than any man."

Garrity followed the tracks until he reached a point where they ended. "The people chasing her must have caught up with the lady right here. There's all sorts of muddling around—and somebody dismounted." He pointed outward. "They rode back toward the main group and must have joined up with them up there a few hundred yards away."

Wildon felt a stab of emotional pain as he realized that a few hours earlier, his beloved Hester had been physically manhandled by a gang of brutes. "Let's get on with it."

The army men traced the hoofmarks back to the main trail. Then the patient tracking began again. Another hour went by before they stopped. This time it was Wildon who called out for a halt. "There's something over there on the horizon to the east."

Garrity expertly slipped out of his stirrups and pulled himself up to stand in the saddle. "Yeah. It's a town. I think we'd better check it out."

"Why?" Wildon asked. "The bandits' trail leads on off to the south."

"Yes, sir," Garrity agreed, dropping back to a sitting position. "But the fact that they passed this close to that settlement shows they weren't worried about the people there. It may be a hangout of theirs."

"Right!" Wildon agreed. "Some of those blackguards might even be there now."

"Could be," Garrity allowed. "Let's pay the place a visit."

"Right, Sergeant."

"We'd best forget the 'sergeant' and 'sir,' Wildon."

"Right you are, Jim."

It took them a half-hour to reach the place. As they rode, the view of the town became clearer. From a smudge it gradually assumed shape until the church steeple was visible. Then a few outlying adobe huts were easily discernible. They spotted a small commercial area along one street.

"There'll be a cantina and a general store along with a couple of other small places," Garrity explained. "Most of these villages are the same."

"You've been down in Mexico before?" Wildon asked.

"Right." Garrity winked at him. "There's been more than once when we were chasing Comanches and conveniently forgot how far south we were."

"I believe that would be termed 'field expediency' at West Point," Wildon said. "Illegal but effective, hey?"

"I hate to admit it, but it wasn't always effective," Garrity said. "But it made the bastards respect and fear us a hell of a lot more."

When they rode into the main street, Wildon saw that Garrity had been correct. A cantina, a general store of sorts, and a couple of small businesses lined the street. The sergeant pointed to the saloon. "That's where we want to go."

They reined up and dismounted. After tying their horses at the hitching rail, Wildon and Garrity walked inside through the open entrance. They brought their long guns in with them. Wildon's eyes darted around restlessly to see if he could spot anyone among the customers resembling any of the raiders he'd traded shots with.

Mismatched tables were arranged around the room. A long bar took up one side of the place, and a door led out toward the rear. Several rough types sat around drinking, and a card game was in progress over in one corner. Garrity chose a table off to one side. They sat down and the sergeant gestured to the barkeep. *"Dos cervezas."* He turned to Wildon. "I just ordered us a couple of beers."

"Well, I am surprised," Wildon said. "I didn't know you could speak Spanish."

"I know enough to enjoy myself," Garrity said.

Wildon pulled some coins out of his pocket and laid them on the table. "Will he take American money?"

"They'll take any kind this close to the border," Garrity said.

The Mexican bartender set two goblets of beer in front of them and pulled out the amount of coins he needed from those on the table. He affected a slight smile. *"Gracias, caballeros."*

Wildon took a sip of the warm beer. "The men in this room appear to be no more than cutthroats."

"That's probably what they are," Garrity agreed. "This part of the country attracts the worst from both the United States and Mexico."

"I should say so. Obviously the fittest and strongest are the survivors here," Wildon said. He carefully studied each man's face. His scrutiny was interrupted by a small hand on his shoulder. He turned around and saw that a small Mexican woman was standing beside him. She smiled and Wildon took off his hat. "How do you do?"

"You looking for a good time, *gringo?*"

"I beg your pardon?"

She playfully nudged him. "Hey, I like you. We go for a good time, eh? One peso *mexicano* or one dollar *americano.*"

"I beg your pardon, miss," Wildon said. He looked

at Garrity. "What is it she wants?"

"She's a whore," Garrity bluntly replied.

Wildon swallowed hard and looked at the visitor to the table as if she were a cross between a reptile and a beautiful flower. "A soiled dove?"

"Yeah. A trollop—a painted lady—whatever you want to call her."

Wildon smiled weakly and looked up at the woman. "Maybe a bit later. I'm looking for somebody."

The girl shrugged and walked over to Garrity. *"Y tu?* What about you, eh?"

Garrity, a professional soldier, was sorely tempted, but he fought down his natural desires. "We'll talk to you later. We are waiting for a friend."

"Esta bien," she said. "I see you later."

She wandered off to the other tables. Wildon turned his attention back to a close study of the cantina's other customers. "Have you seen anyone that appears to have been among the raiders?" he asked.

Garrity shook his head. "Nope. But if I was you, I wouldn't stare quite so hard."

"I don't feel the need for a display of proper etiquette," Wildon whispered sharply. "My wife has been kidnapped. I don't care a hang if I offend one of these ruffians." He continued his searching gaze until a man from a table across the room stood up and walked over to them.

"Para que buscas?" he asked. He was a mestizo dressed in vaquero style. The pistol and large knife in his belt seemed as natural a part of him as his hands. "You t'ink I am pretty?"

Garrity interjected here. "My *amigo* is looking for an *hombre* that owes him *dinero. Mucho dinero.* He is not looking at you."

Wildon's temper, frayed from the strain he was under, heated up. "I most certainly do not think you are pretty."

"Oh? Then you t'ink I am *feo,* eh?"

Wildon looked at Garrity, "What is *feo?*"

"It means ugly," Garrity said. "Now it would—"

"Yes, indeed," Wildon said to the man. "You are *feo.* As a matter of fact I have never in all my life seen such a *feo* person as you."

The vaquero stepped back, his hand dropping to his holster. He slipped his pistol free, but a blast from Garrity's gun sounded. The mestizo back-stepped and sat down on the floor. He looked up at Wildon and spat blood straight at him. Then he fell backward dead.

More shots sounded in the cantina. Wildon, acting under blind instinct and fear, now had his Remington out. He fired without aiming across the room. But Garrity's shooting was of a more serious nature.

Two men on the other side went down. Now Wildon noticed they had been firing at them. A movement off to one side caught his eye, and he looked to see the bartender aiming a shotgun toward him and Garrity. He aimed at the man and fired twice. The Mexican's face seemed to suddenly collapse inward; then the man disappeared from view as he collapsed.

The prostitute emitted a loud scream. *"Ya matastes a mi esposo!"*

"What's she shouting about?" Wildon asked over the roaring of the guns.

"You just killed her husband," Garrity said.

Wildon's mind, although thoroughly occupied by the present gun battle, felt shock at the revelation.

The drinkers who had been in the middle of the fracas were on the floor. Most were scurrying on their hands and knees toward the exit. The ones on the far side, including the half-dozen card players, had joined the gunfight. "I'm sounding Recall," Garrity said. "Let's get the hell out of here." He'd reholstered his pistol and had gone to the Henry repeater.

Wildon followed his example, pumping his Winchester and pulling the trigger to send three heavy slugs streaking toward the hostile crowd across the cantina. One man fell forward to the floor while another grabbed his arm and spun around. The firing had enough effect on the others to make them scramble away.

Wildon and Garrity, still firing, broke for the door. They charged outside, not letting up in their shooting in order to discourage any potential assassins in that direction. The cavalrymen bolted aboard their horses and turned for a run out of the village. They rode hard and fast, putting as much distance as possible between them and the death scene.

Wildon, realizing his inexperience, followed Garrity. They pounded toward the mountains, keeping the horses going all out for another fifteen minutes before settling down into a ground-eating canter.

"We're lucky it's so close to dark," Garrity said.

"Damnation!" Wildon said. "I wasn't expecting that."

"Most of 'em had been drinking," Garrity told him. "If they hadn't been, we'd be with the other dead men."

Wanting to spare their horses as much as possible, they slowed down even more. Several glances back showed they were not being followed.

"Lieutenant Boothe, I want to explain something to you," Garrity said. "It ain't considered polite out here to stare at folks. They take it as nosiness or a challenge. Particularly like an invitation to trouble."

"It is a lesson I have quickly learned," Wildon said. "This subculture in which we are traveling is completely alien to anything I've ever known in the past. I promise, Sergeant, that in future I shall practice more discretion."

"Does that mean not attracting attention to yourself?"

"In this case, yes!" Wildon said.

"Fine." He pointed to the mountains. "We can find a place to hole up for the rest of the night. Then we'll get back to tracking down the bandits."

Wildon nodded. The sudden thought of Hester away from him and in the hands of men like those in the cantina chilled his heart.

CHAPTER 10

Hester Boothe almost jumped from the wicker chair she was sitting in when the door to the room abruptly opened. The older woman she'd seen earlier in the day entered carrying a dress. Hester looked closely at the oldster but could not figure out what race or nationality she was. Although she was dark complected and her gray hair was in braids like Indian women depicted in lithographs, she wore a gaily colored dress with a white apron. Her feet were adorned by leather sandals.

The woman spoke in a raspy voice. *"Cambiate pronto!"* She tossed the dress at Hester, then turned and walked away, slamming the door.

Assuming the short statement to be a command to change into the garment, Hester angrily threw it aside without as much as a cursory examination. She continued to sit in the chair, staring at the wall. A short time passed when the woman again appeared. She frowned when she saw the dress lying on the floor. *"No te gusta, gringita? Y que importa. Venga."* She gestured in a way that made Hester think she wanted her to go away. But after a few moments she realized the woman wanted her to follow.

Hester, a fresh feeling of fear rising in her, kept to the chair. She looked away as a silent sign she had no intention of following the woman.

"Que tienes?" the oldster asked. *"Venga. El general y tu van a comer."* She shuffled over to Hester and nudged her.

"Leave me alone!"

"Pandeja!" The woman grabbed Hester and pulled her from the chair. *"Venga!"*

Hester resisted, but the woman was surprisingly strong for her age. The American finally decided there was no use in resisting. She walked slowly after the woman into the next room. The delicious smell of strange food was strong as she went through the door. There was a large table with a white tablecloth covered with plates, silverware, and serving dishes. There were also some silver goblets and several bottles of wine. Hester suddenly realized how hungry she was.

The old woman pointed to each dish and spoke to identify its contents. *"Tamales. Frijolitos con queso. Chiles jalapeños. Vino,"* she said. *"Son muy deliciosos."* She pulled a chair out from the table. *"Sientete."*

Hester figured she was to sit down. She numbly complied, enjoying the aroma coming from the food. The old woman looked her over carefully, then left her alone. Hester tried to straighten out some of the wrinkles in the calico dress. The days in the wagon and the wild horseback ride earlier had left it a mess. She vaguely wondered what sort of

102

garment she had just thrown to the floor. It had been emerald green and carefully folded.

The door opened once again, but this time it was not the woman. It was Hubert Mauveaux. He was dressed in a colorful uniform. The tunic was a dark blue with a high red collar and epaulets. A single gold stripe lined the lower cuff while a fancy scroll design ran up each sleeve. The trousers were bright red with a wide gold stripe up the sides. The effect was finished off with a pair of extremely shiny black boots and a kepi. The headgear was similar to that of the American army except it was darker and red on top with gold striping. He bowed and clicked his heels. Although not a handsome man, there was the aura of a *chevalier* about him in the way he conducted himself and moved about. He had a grace that spoke of serious social training sometime in his life.

"Bonsoir, madame." He had also shaved, oiled his hair, and waxed his mustache to curly magnificence.

"Bonsoir, monsieur," Hester replied in a sullen voice.

His eyes widened and a wide smile stretched across his aquiline features. *"Vous parlez francais!"*

"Yes, *monsieur*, I speak French," she replied in the language. "And again I must insist on my immediate release."

Mauveaux ignored her stern plea. "It is more than I could have hoped and dreamed for, *madame!* A beautiful lady who is educated and cultured and—" He stopped speaking and clasped his hands in distress. *"Je regrette!* I did not properly introduce myself to you."

"You've already told me who you are," Hester said coldly.

"But that was out there and I was dressed as a common man." Mauveaux walked over and grasped her hand before she could pull back. He kissed it, saying, "I am Hubert Mauveaux, *ex-sous lieutenant du Regiment des Chasseurs d'Afrique* of the French Colonial Army."

"And I am still Mrs. Boothe, wife of Lieutenant Boothe of the United States Cavalry."

"Ah! Again I must seek your forgiveness, *madame!* I did not offer you any wine." He poured her a glassful, then served himself. "This is wine of California," he said. "Although a bit crude in comparison to the vintages of my native France, I feel that in time the Californians may equal or surpass the Old World." He tinkled a bell. "Shall we eat?"

The old lady appeared. *"Si, General Don Humberto?"*

"Serveinos, por favor," he said.

The old woman shuffled to the table to fill their plates. After setting the platters down in front of them she made a silent exit.

"That is *Señora* Gonzales," he explained. "Although an illiterate, she performs her household duties most remarkably. You may have picked up the fact she addressed me as 'general.' That is because I am in command of this army outside my castle."

"It is a small army," Hester said.

"You have not seen all of it, *madame*, nor do you realize its potential," Mauveaux said. He noted that Hester took a bite of the food. "And how is your meal, *madame?*"

"Fine, thank you," Hester said. The food was actually better than anything she had eaten at Fort MacNeil or on the wagon train. Between it and Mauveaux's impeccable manners, she began to feel some confidence. She thought it best to keep the conversation on the pleasant side. "Your housekeeper told me the names of these dishes, but I cannot recall."

"She told you in Spanish, no doubt," Mauveaux said. "What you are eating now is called a *tamale*. It is beef, olives, and flavorings wrapped in a cornmeal paste, then baked. The other is the form of Mexican beans with a special goat cheese on the top. You seem to find the food to your liking."

"It is delicious," Hester replied. "And what is in that bowl?"

"Ah! Take care, *madame!* That is a fiery food called *jalapeños!* It takes time to get used to them," Mauveaux cautioned her. He picked one of the large green peppers and ate it, smiling in a superior manner.

Hester, feeling defiant, reached out and took one. She bit down, immediately feeling the fiery juices fill her mouth. But she continued to eat it slowly, as if savoring the taste. The only outward sign of distress were the tears in her eyes. She dabbed at them with her napkin after finishing the pepper. Although her voice was a bit strained, she had it under control. "Most interesting."

"You are a remarkable woman!" he exclaimed.

The meal lasted an hour and a half. They ate slowly and sipped the wine while Mauveaux told her of his home in Orleans and a bit about his cold father and eccentric mother.

"I have inherited her passions," he said. "I, too, am a romanticist with a tender heart full of passion and love."

"How do you know this of your mother, *monsieur?*" Hester asked.

"It was no secret that she was unfaithful to my father and had many lovers. I know, for I saw several myself."

Hester, an Anglo-Saxon raised in that race's environ of womanly chastity and modesty, gasped in surprise at this casual revelation of his mother's adulterous conduct.

But Mauveaux did not notice. He continued talking, enjoying this chance to converse in his native tongue. After years of border women who lacked any exposure to life's more refined aspects, the Frenchman was fast falling deeper in love with the beautiful American woman with her obvious social graces. His conversation was disjointed in his excitement as he went from subject to subject. At one point he interrupted himself in mid-sentence. "How disappointed I am, *madame!*"

"Why is that, *monsieur?*" Hester asked.

"I made you a gift of a beautiful dress, but you did not choose to wear it," he said.

"Monsieur," Hester said almost defiantly, "I am a married woman, and I do not accept gifts from strange gentlemen. In my circle it would be considered most inappropriate and improper conduct."

"But of course! But I am not a stranger to you," Mauveaux explained. "We have been introduced, and now we are dining together on fine food in a wonderful atmosphere. And there is more." He turned toward the door, snapping his fingers. "Julio! *Venga por favor.*"

A Mexican man carrying a violin came into the room. He bowed and, without further ceremony, began to play Chopin's "Polonaise." Now Hester had to admit that the music was also better than what she'd heard at Fort MacNeil. She took another sip of wine, not realizing she was beginning to get a little drunk.

The violinist went through a half-dozen pieces before he ended his concert. After bowing again to their applause, he made a graceful exit.

"How wonderful!" Hester exclaimed. "Where on earth did you find him?"

"His name is Julio Montenegro, and he once played the first violin in the Mexico City symphonic orchestra," Mauveaux explained. "But he murdered a man and was forced to flee the capital. Eventually he joined up with my army and acquired a violin during a raid on a hacienda in Sonora. After I heard him play, I made sure he would do nothing to risk his life or his hands. He is one of the permanent guards left here at our mountain fortress."

"Remarkable!" Hester said, fascinated. "And he is a murderer?"

"This is the New World, *madame,*" Mauveaux explained. "In building empires, one must deal with various elements of undesirables from time to time."

"You are forging an empire, *monsieur?*" Hester asked.

"But of course! This uniform I wear may be that of a lieutenant, but an emperor's robes shall be mine one day," Mauveaux said. "I shall take up where Maximilian left off."

"As I recall," Hester said pointedly, "Maximilian was executed by the Mexicans."

"He was not a true emperor, *madame*," Mauveaux replied. "He depended on the goodwill and support of others. I shall do my own empire building."

"I wish you luck," Hester said.

"Would you not wish to be my empress?" Mauveaux asked. "Together we would rule over a dominion that would stretch from the American border down to Tierra del Fuego. Two continents!"

"No, thank you," Hester said smiling.

"*Madame*, you cut me deeply!" the Frenchman exclaimed. "How can you be so cruel to one who loves you passionately?"

Hester became flustered. The man had not spoken of loving her, and she was unprepared for such unwelcome attention. She reverted to English. "Sir! How many times must I tell you that I am a married woman?"

"I love you with all my heart!" Mauveaux cried out. He went to her and sank down to one knee. "My soul calls out for you."

"Good Lord!"

"I cannot go on without you," Mauveaux insisted. "When I saw you standing beside that wagon, my passions and affections boiled over. I had to have you as my own."

"You kidnapped me, sir! I was forced to go with you against my will, and I strongly resent it," Hester said. "You have made me a most unhappy prisoner."

"Oh, no, *madame!* It is I who is the prisoner — *un prisonnier d'amour!*"

"I demand my release," Hester said. "If you have no consideration for me, please think of my poor husband."

The expression on Mauveaux's face darkened. "I hate him! The jealousy I feel courses through my body like a hot fire." He looked passionately and longingly into her face. "He has had you and I have not!"

"And, sir, you shall not!" Hester exclaimed.

"You torture me with your beauty!"

With the effect of the wine swirling in her head, Hester got unsteadily to her feet. "I demand that you take me back to my husband."

"My heart demands that you surrender to me," Mauveaux countered. He rushed over and put his arms around her waist. "Give yourself to me, *mon petit chou.*"

"Don't call me you little cabbage!" Hester said. "I am Wildon's little cabbage." Her wine-muddled mind then considered what a strange term of affection that was.

"I will make you love me," Mauveaux promised. "You will be mine through our mortal lives and eternity too. The people will call you their empress."

"I would rather live with my husband on officers' row than with you in a golden palace!" Hester said.

"Tell me your name," he begged.

"Mrs. Wildon Boothe," Hester replied.

"No, *ma fleur!* Your Christian name," Mauveaux insisted.

"I certainly shall not," Hester said, moving toward the other door.

"Then I shall give you one," he said. The Frenchman stopped his amorous attentions as he turned his thoughts to an appropriate appellation for the woman he now felt would sit by his side as he ruled his New World empire. *"Alons!* I have it. You shall be *L'Impératrice* Camille — the Empress Camille. Your beautiful face and lovely figure fit that name perfectly."

"I am," Hester insisted loudly, "Mrs. Wildon Boothe!" She fled the room, going through the door and slamming it shut. She looked frantically for some way to bolt it shut, but could find none. But her unwanted host made no effort to force it open.

Mauveaux spoke to her from the door. "I am a patient man, *ma chère* Camille! You will be mine — one way or the other!"

CHAPTER 11

The trail had stopped cold.

Garrity, kneeling down for a closer look at the ground, finally gave it up. He got to his feet and shrugged. "The terrain is too rocky here. It would take an Apache scout to figure out the marks and scratches."

They had spent the whole day following the track that grew more and more difficult to see. From distinct hoofmarks, the spoor had disintegrated to mere marks and scratches on the ground. Finally, even that poor sign disappeared as the hard terrain became smooth and virtually unmarked.

It was now early evening, and it seemed the many hours spent on the trail had been for nothing. Wildon looked around at the mountains to the south. A feeling of utter hopelessness swept over him.

"There are at least a thousand different routes to the summits. And we don't know which one holds our quarry." He angrily hit the saddle horn with his fist. "It seems so impossible now. Look at the vastness of this place. My God! It is endless."

"There's an advantage to that. We can see a hell

of a long way in country like this. I'll admit it will take time, sir," Garrity said. "But we'll pull it off."

Wildon sighed. "I just hope we do have time."

"Those outlaws might not have even gone that way," Garrity said. "They could have turned off east and headed for Chihuahua. But we can find them there too."

Wildon felt helpless in spite of the sergeant's optimism. "Is there any chance they might have gone west?"

"I doubt it," Garrity said. "There's not too many places to hole up out in the desert. And the Yaqui Injuns own that particular piece of the earth. Nobody, not even a bandit gang, would want to tangle with that tribe."

"What do you suggest?"

"We could waste a lot of time going the wrong way," Garrity said. "It might be a good idea to hunt up another settlement and do some inquiring."

"I'll mind my manners this time," Wildon said. "God! It makes me sick to think of how I spoiled our visit in that cantina. We might have learned something."

"Maybe not," Garrity said, getting up into his saddle. "Let's not fret over that. The best course of action would be to act like we're looking for employment. A border gang can always use another coupla guns."

"Then we shall play the role of desperados, hey?"

"That's it, sir," Garrity said. "But don't try to pass yourself off as a man who's been out here a long time."

Wildon smiled. "I'm still quite the Easterner, am

I?"

"Sir, you sure as hell are," Garrity said. "But we can say you were in trouble with the law back there and ended up on the Mexican border. Let's pretend we joined up together a while back and have had some bad luck."

"I understand."

The two cavalrymen changed direction and rode out of the foothills. The horses seemed to appreciate the easier terrain, and they picked up a bit of speed without being goaded into it. It took an hour to reach the flatlands again. Garrity led them to the southeast, riding easily, still looking for the bandit trail in case they might stumble across something. But the ground stayed barren of telltale sign. After another half-hour, Wildon called out.

"Sergeant! Look to the horizon on our left."

Garrity looked in that direction. At first he saw nothing, but finally he caught sight of a wisp of smoke carried upward and whipped away. "Nice job, sir. Let's go over that way and see what's going on."

Soon after they settled in for the ride, the horses again picked up speed. Garrity knew the reason. "They smell fresh water."

Giving the animals their own lead, the two cavalrymen settled in for the ride. A few minutes later they could see the settlement nestled on the banks of a narrow river. The sergeant knew exactly what lay ahead. "There's some adobe huts and fields," he said. "We won't find a cantina there, but maybe the folks will help us get back on the right track."

Their welcome into the village was not particularly warm. The men were outside the huts. Garrity knew the women and children would be inside. These were people that had experienced bad treatment from strangers in the past. He chose a middle-aged man who seemed to be the leader. Garrity nodded.

"Buenos noches, señor."

The man, unsmiling, answered with a nod.

"We are looking for *hombres bandidos,*" Garrity said in a mixture of Spanish and English. "Maybe *doce* or *trece* of them. There is a *mujer americana* with them."

"I don't see no *bandidos,*" the Mexican said. "I don't see no *gringa* neither."

Garrity pointed to the mountains. "They live in *las montañas* someplace. Do you know where?"

"No, *señor.*"

Wildon looked at the man. "You must help us, sir!"

The man shrugged. *"Por que?* If you want the *bandidos,* look for them."

"We are, *señor,*" Garrity said. He knew the bandits were feared and hated by the villagers. It seemed that veracity was the best course. "The *mujer americana* is my friend's wife."

"The *bandidos* take a lot of men's wives," the Mexican said. "That is nothing new."

"Cobardes!" The shrill cry of the woman's voice broke into the scene.

Wildon and Garrity looked over to see a young woman step from one of the huts. She looked at the men and spat. Then she walked over to Wildon.

114

"I speak English. I work in the house of Americans in San Antonio for two years."

"I hope you can help us," Wildon said.

"I hear you say the bad men take your wife," the woman said. "It is true what Clemente say about they take lots of wives." She glared at the Mexican, then turned back to the young officer. "But at least you go to get yours back. You do not act like she has been soiled and is too unclean for you."

Wildon didn't like the way the conversation was going. "I'd rather not—"

She interrupted him. "The men you look for are led by an evil one called Humberto Movo." She pointed. "Look to the south. See the highest mountain with the flat top? That is where they live. It is the part of the range called the Santo Domingos. The mountain you seek is *Montaña Bandido*—Bandit Mountain."

The one she pointed out was easy to see. Tall and craggy, the apex seemed flattened as if some giant's hand had pressed down on it.

"Thank you very much," Wildon said.

"Movo and his devils only come out to kill and rob," the woman said. "My own dear sister died of their outrages." She turned and sneered at the village spokesman. "And this one abandoned his wife of five years because she was raped."

The man stepped forward, tears in his eyes, and hit the young woman so hard that she fell to the ground. *"Callate!"* he bellowed at her. *"Sangrona de tu madre!"*

Wildon was angered by the man's action. "Don't do that again, sir. I warn you!"

115

The Mexican looked at the Americans. "What is a man to do? Did it not tear out my heart to have her taken by other men?" He glared at Wildon. "What are you going to do, *señor? Dime*—tell me! What are you going to do?"

"Let's go, Sergeant," Wildon said. He pulled on his horse's reins and kicked the animal into a gallop. As they rode back into the desert, the Mexican woman's voice sounded above their mounts' hooves.

"I will pray for help from all the saints to guide you. *Vaya con Dios*—Go with God!"

Wildon and Garrity had ridden until darkness forced them to stop. Sullen and sad, the lieutenant had not eaten the night before. Garrity, sympathizing with him, knew there was nothing he could say. Their camp that night was a quiet somber bivouac.

The next morning, up in the dawn's penetrating chill, they took time only for some hot coffee. After quickly downing the brew, they pulled themselves up into their saddles for a long day of riding.

"We'll make better time today," the sergeant said. "We won't be following any trails."

Wildon, anxious to get on with the task, looked far across the flat terrain to the smudge of mountains in the distance. "How long do you figure it will be before we reach the Santo Domingos?"

Garrity, the old soldier, judged the distance with an instinct born of years of active campaigning. "Just a bit before dark."

"Damn!" Wildon said. "I was hoping we could get there with enough time to get something accom-

116

plished."

"We'll be arriving at the right time, Lieutenant," Garrity assured him. "We'll be able to settle in, then maybe do a little scouting before dark. We can spend tomorrow giving the place a good look-over."

"The whole day? I would certainly like to have my wife out of there as quickly as possible." •

"First we got to find out exactly where she is, sir," Garrity said. "If we can find a way to observe for a while, we might just be able to spot her."

Wildon appreciated the older man's wisdom. "Thank you, Sergeant. Let's ride."

They traveled through the entire morning. The only rests the horses got were when the two men dismounted and led them. Normal horses might have become dangerously fatigued, but the oat-fed, well-conditioned mounts of the United States Cavalry responded to the good treatment they had received with stamina, strength, and a willingness to obey.

Finally, however, in early afternoon, the soldiers called a halt. Even healthy animals have limits. Especially if great demands might be put on them in the near future.

Removing the saddles, they allowed the animals a brief rest. Curry brushes came out of the saddlebags and a good brushing down aided in restoring some vitality. After an hour, the equipment was thrown aboard once more, and the trek resumed.

Wildon was gratified to see that the shadowy images of the Santo Domingos had begun to show some clarity. Cuts and ravines in the sides of the mountains was evident as were other features. Garrity, on the other hand, had something else catch his attention.

"There's a man ahead, sir," Garrity said, pulling his field glasses from their case wrapped around the saddle horn. "He's on foot and leading a horse."

By then Wildon had his own binoculars up to his eyes. "The animal is lame." He studied the man for a few moments. "By golly! I think the fellow is one of the bandits!"

"You're right about that, sir."

"Then let's ride up there and grab the rascal, Sergeant!"

"Hold up, Lieutenant," Garrity cautioned him. He gave the surrounding area a good scrutiny. "There doesn't seem to be any of his pards nearby. They probably left him to get back on his own." He looked at the lieutenant. "Let's make a quiet approach."

"Right."

They increased the pace without forcing the mounts into a gallop. It took three quarters of an hour to get close enough to use the naked eye to be able to tell what sort of clothing the bandit wore. "Hold up, sir," Garrity said, reining in.

Curious, Wildon glanced over at the sergeant and brought his own mount to a stop.

Garrity calmly pulled the Henry rifle from the saddle boot. He aimed carefully, then gently squeezed the trigger. The rifle recoiled backward into his shoulder.

"Nice shooting, Sergeant!" Wildon exclaimed.

Up ahead, the bandit looked down at the horse that lay dead at his feet. He quickly glanced back and saw the two Americans who were now riding hell-for-leather toward him. Panic-stricken, the man ran toward the mountains. Garrity, in the lead, bore down on him. When he caught up, the sergeant slapped the man on the back of the head and sent him tumbling. He brought his horse to a halt, leaping off and rushing up to the fallen bandit.

Garrity reached the man who had now gotten up on his knees. He hit the desperado straight in the face, knocking him onto his back.

Wildon now joined them. He also swung out of the saddle, but wisely left the formalities to the N.C.O.

The bandit sat up, rubbing his jaw. "Hey! You're no *amigable,* eh?"

"Damned right I ain't," Garrity said. "Get up."

The bandit shook his head. "No. You only want to hit me again."

Garrity brandished the rifle. "Get up or I'm gonna lay this rifle across your skull."

"Espera!" the bandit asked. He got to his feet, cringing as he expected another blow. When nothing happened, he relaxed. "What you want, eh? I ain't got no money."

"I want to know where you're taking the American girl," Garrity said.

"I don't know nothing about no 'merican *muchacha,*" the bandit insisted.

Garrity exploded into action, crashing the barrel of the Henry against the man's arm. He looked down on the now fallen man. "Tell me about her."

"I don't know nothing." The second blow rolled him over. "Goddamn! *Calmate!*"

"I'll damned well beat you to death," Garrity said. "I know you're from Movo's gang."

The bandit held his arm that was obviously broken. "Don't hit me no more, man. I tell you right out. I am one of Mauveaux's men."

Wildon, without realizing it himself, suddenly moved. He kicked the bandit in the midsection while pulling his hunting knife from its scabbard. He bent down and held the blade to the man's throat. "The American woman is my wife."

The bandit swallowed. "I guess you want her back, eh?"

"Tell me where to find her or I'll cut your goddamned throat," Wildon said coolly.

"She was grabbed by Mauveaux," the bandit said. "He rode up to her and picked her up. She tried to get away once, but he caught her. I ain't seen the 'merican *muchacha* since my horse went lame."

"Tell me the exact location of the bandit camp," Wildon said.

The bandit pointed over his shoulder. "You can see the mountain with the flat top? That is where it is."

Wildon increased the pressure of the knife. "Tell me exactly where it is situated."

"On the top, the whole top," the bandit said. "That's *exactamente* where. Easy with *el cuchillo*—the knife."

Wildon pushed the man away and stood up. "That's what the girl back in the farming village said."

"That's about all we can learn from this sonofabitch," Garrity said. He put the Henry to his shoulder and aimed at the bandit.

"Oh, shit!" the bandit said, crossing himself.

"What the hell are you going to do, Sergeant?" Wildon demanded to know.

"I'm going to shoot this feller," Garrity said in a matter-of-fact tone.

"No! I won't have cold-blooded murder," Wildon insisted.

"Sir!" Garrity protested.

"That's an order, Sergeant."

"Sir, he's gonna pop up later to haunt us," Wildon said. "He's a goddamned devil. The world is better without him."

The bandit looked at Wildon. "Don't let him kill me!"

"Leave him be," Wildon said. "He'll be alone and on foot in the wild country."

"Lieutenant, that bastard could walk through hell and back again if he had to," Garrity pointed out.

"Let's go, Sergeant." Wildon walked over and stepped up into his saddle.

Shaking his head, Garrity walked over to his mount.

CHAPTER 12

Garrity looked back at Wildon and pointed to the ground. "Here's the trail we lost, sir. It's popped up again in this softer ground."

Wildon glanced downward, recognizing the marks they had spend so much time trailing but had lost when the terrain turned rockier. They led straight to a path that ascended into the boulders above. The military side of his mind spoke out.

"I would imagine that track is well guarded," he said. "It certainly would be if I were charged with its defense."

"Yes, sir," Garrity said. "The bandits will have a series of guard posts all the way up there to the entrance of their camp. It's something they picked up from Injuns. The only difference is that picket duty is voluntary in the tribes. I'd be willing to bet the bandit leader makes sure this place is secured proper." He indicated another area that offered a way to the top. This was trackless country, strewn with boulders. "It'll take longer, but it's a guarantee we'll at least make it."

"Isn't there a chance of patrols?" Wildon asked.

Garrity nodded. "There sure is, sir, and we'd

better be ready for them." He loosened the pistol in his holster. "Ready to go?"

Wildon followed his example, but also pulled his Winchester up a couple of inches. "I'll be using this if we have an unexpected meeting."

"Good idea, sir," Garrity said. "But it'll take both hands on the reins to handle these animals. That's pretty steep terrain there." He urged his horse forward and, with Wildon close behind, began the slow ascent.

The mountain side offered more problems other than its steep angle. Large boulders, some piled on top of others, were packed close together. On several occasions, the two riders were forced to back down or turn around when what promised to be a good avenue to the top turned out to be a dead end.

The horses, good military mounts, did as well as possible as their hooves clattered over the rocky ground. They snorted and strained, doing the duty required of them. Finally Wildon and Garrity, both dedicated horsemen and cavalry soldiers, put the condition of their animals ahead of everything else.

"If we don't give 'em a breather, they'll bust their hearts," Garrity said.

Wildon leaned forward a bit and patted his horse on the neck. "These fine fellows deserve some consideration."

They dismounted and led the steeds by the reins,

taking away most of the physical strain for the noble beasts.

Several times, Garrity left his horse with Wildon and went ahead on foot to check out a potential pathway. If it was a good one, he came back and got his horse to continue the climb. If not, he tried other approaches until he found one that would take them higher toward the objective.

Three hours of the strenuous work was exhausting. Soaked in sweat and breathing hard from the exertion, Wildon and Garrity had to rest. But it would have been foolhardy to relax in the open. After a half-hour of searching, they found some cover back in a small tree-filled ravine. The cavalrymen wanted only to sit down and let their fatigue-cramped muscles relax. Once they were inside the small grove of trees, they found something else — a stream of cool water.

Trickling down from above, the little creek was not more than a foot wide. They first saw to it that their faithful mounts got all of the refreshing liquid they wanted. After the horses had slaked their thirst, the two soldiers thought of their own physical comfort. Garrity stuck his face in the water and drank long and deep.

"You'd better take it easy, Sergeant," Wildon cautioned him. "You're supposed to drink sparingly when you're hot and thirsty. That's one thing I did learn at West Point."

Garrity shook his head. "Pardon me, Lieutenant, but that's so much hog swill. I've heard that for years, but a few summers of campaigning has taught me differ'nt. That includes this part of the country for quite a few years and some real blistering weather from Virginia down to Georgia. That experience taught me that when the temperature is up, it's a big help to fill yourself with water. You're dried out and you need it." The sergeant went back to his hard consumption from the stream.

Wildon joined him, at first trying to drink a little bit. But within moments, he was gulping it down as fast as the sergeant. He finally had his fill. "Damn," he sighed. "That does feel better, doesn't it?"

"Never argue with an old sergeant," Garrity said, winking at the young lieutenant. He pointed upward to where the source of the water that trickled into the ravine would be located. "Clear, cold water like this comes from a mountain spring. When we get to the top, we can use the pool to drink out of. That'll be where this stuff is coming from. And we can follow the stream straight up."

Their canteens had been filled from the river by the farming village. The water was warm and stale. They poured it out and refilled the containers. Finally refreshed and feeling good, the two soldiers took their horses' reins and resumed the tortuous route to the top of Bandido Mountain.

* * *

Hester watched dully as *Señora* Gonzales supervised the other two Mexican women. They dragged a heavy copper bathtub into the room. The old woman issued some quick orders and her charges scurried away. She went to a cupboard in the corner of the room and took out a large thick towel, a washcloth, and a bar of soap. She laid them on a chair by the tub.

Moments later the other two returned with pots of hot water. They poured the water into the tub and went out for more. When it was full, they withdrew. *Señora* Gonzales nodded to Hester. *"Ahorra, bañate, gringita."* Then she walked out of the room and closed the door.

Hester looked at the inviting bath, hot and steamy, with the soap and towels nearby. The thought of slipping into the water almost made her swoon. She walked over and stood beside the tub. She knew that the week on the wagon train and the wild ride up the mountain had left her sweaty and sticky. But she also knew that to bathe and refresh herself would make her more desirable to the love-mad Mauveaux. A chance existed also that he might suddenly appear in the room while she was naked and vulnerable.

Hester decided against a full bath, but she gave in enough to wash her face and hands. She bent down and picked up the soap. She gasped when she saw its brand name was Bristol. This sign from home made her feel sentimental and sad. Slowly, she dipped her hands into the bath and wet her face. Then, using the washcloth, she carefully washed.

When Hester finished, she felt much better even with that small amount of bathing. She walked to the barred window of the room and gazed up at the wall of boulders that surrounded the bandit camp. The realization that the route to Wildon and freedom was just on the other side was a tantalizing, emotional torture.

Hester stood gazing outward for a long time while the shadows lengthened across the interior of the settlement. A sudden wave of grief swept over her, and she wept silently in despair and frustration. The melancholy feeling was abruptly swept away by the sudden sound of feminine voices in the other room. Hester wiped at her eyes with the sleeve of her dress. Two women were approaching the door, their rapid speech growing louder. She recognized one as *Señora* Gonzales, but the other was that of a much younger woman—and it was shrill with bristling anger.

The door burst open and the two women entered. The younger was the beautiful, svelte Mexican woman Hester had seen when she was brought into the camp. She glared at the American, her hands on her hip in a challenging manner.

"*Yo soy* Lola—I am Lola!"

The old woman grabbed Lola's arm and pulled

at her, muttering angrily in Spanish.

Lola pushed *Señora* Gonzales away. The old woman persisted in trying to pull her from the room. With growing irritation, Lola turned and grabbed her and, shoving her through the door, slammed it shut with a vicious push. The house-keeper yelled from the other room; then her foot-steps could be heard scurrying away. Lola walked boldly into the room, striding around and around Hester. She pointed to the bath water. "Hey! You don't like to be clean?"

Hester, fearless, stood her ground. "Is there something I might do for you?"

Lola grabbed her nose. *"Que pistosa!* You stink!"

This was worse than anything that had happened to her. It was a real insult to her dignity from a social inferior. Hester's hand lashed out, striking Lola in the face. "Shut your mouth, you miserable wench!"

"Ay!" Lola cried out, holding her stung cheek. "I get you for that, *gringa!"* She charged forward and grabbed Hester. "I make you sorry you take my Humberto!"

Hester grasped the Mexican woman and swung her around. Both went down and rolled across the floor, screaming and clawing at each other. Lola ended up on top, but Hester remembered seeing her boy cousins wrestle and recalled a trick they used to employ when one had pinned down the other. She swung one leg up and locked it around Lola's face and pulled her down and off her. Reacting quickly, Hester sat up and jumped on her adversary.

Señora Gonzales, with two men from the settlement, rushed back into the room, screaming hysterically. Laughing, the bandits pulled Hester free, then grabbed Lola and dragged her toward the door screaming in rage. The shrieking continued all the way through the next room and out into the hall.

Hester ran to the barred window and looked down in the darkening compound to see Lola still being pulled away. Hester took a deep breath and shouted, "Let that be a lesson to you! We Bristol women are fighters!"

The old woman, slowly shaking her head, looked at Hester. *"Ya ahorra tienes una enimiga bien peligrosa*—now you got bad enemy!"

Wildon and Garrity led their horses back into a small box canyon. Its fifty-yard length curved slightly around to a point that concealed the back from the entrance.

"This may be home for a few days, sir," Garrity said. "So let's make it comfortable and safe. The first thing to do is take some branches, and brush away our tracks leading into here."

"Right," Wildon agreed. "I'll take care of that."

"Fine, sir," Garrity said. "I'll fix up some brush here so's we can't be spotted from above. Then we'll take a look around."

The chore took a quarter of an hour. It had grown much darker by the time they finished. Wildon glanced upward at the sky. "That full moon is mighty bright."

"Just what the doctor ordered, sir," Garrity said. "It's giving off enough light to make a reconnaissance mission possible."

After making sure their horses were comfortable, the two cavalrymen set out on foot to ascend to a point of observation on the bandit camp perimeter. It was easy to move silently through the rocks. The large formations were close together, offering good footholds. When they reached the top, they found they could peer straight down into the settlement.

Garrity tapped Wildon's shoulder. "There's a good place over there, sir." He pointed to a place where a large, flat-topped boulder slanted upward.

"Let's perch awhile," Wildon suggested.

The pair crossed a couple of ledges, then stepped onto the slab of rock. Lying down, they crawled up to the edge and gazed down on what was really a small town.

"Jesus!" Garrity said. "There's a lot o' them bastards, ain't there?"

"There certainly is, Sergeant," Wildon said. "They didn't have a quarter of their full strength with them during the attack on the baggage train."

"That shows that whoever's running that outfit has military training," Garrity said. "He knew how many wagons and men we had."

"There's no doubt about it," Wildon said. "He probably scouted us first. I wonder why none of our flankers spotted them."

"Fellers like that have spent their whole lives sneaking around," Garrity said. "Hunting as youngsters, then fighting as full-growed men. They do it so much it becomes second nature with 'em."

"They're good all right," Wildon allowed.

"Yes, sir. And their leader took the right amount of men to do the job. The only thing he didn't know was that we wasn't carrying nothing worth the effort. Mulvaney told us he saw 'em look in the wagons."

"Lord above!" Wildon exclaimed. "It gives you chills, doesn't it? They could have wiped us all out."

"It means, Lieutenant, that getting your missus outta there is gonna be that much harder," Garrity said. "But we'll do it."

"Damned right we will, Sergeant," Wildon said.

They spent a half-hour watching the activities of the town. The one large building in the center dominated the scene. Garrity studied it for a while. "That's gotta be their headquarters," he concluded.

"That's where they'll have Hester," Wildon said.

"Maybe," Garrity said. He wanted to say that it depended on which bandit owned her, but he didn't see the point in adding to the officer's misery.

Sudden shouting broke out by one of the huts. The two soldiers looked over and saw a pair of bandits yelling and gesturing at each other. One went for his pistol, working smooth and fast, shooting the other one down. A few others came up, and the arguing continued until more shots exploded over the scene. The episode ended with a total of three bodies sprawled in front of the hut.

"Cold-blooded bastards," Garrity remarked.

"God!" Wildon said. "We've got to get Hester out of there quick."

Garrity noticed something else. "There's an entrance in the rocks down there to the left. See?"

Wildon peered intently. "Right! It's big enough to ride horses through." He looked at Garrity. "You appear to have formulated a plan."

"I think we should pull out of here now and get a good night's rest," Garrity suggested. "This place is hidden enough that we can spend all day tomorrow keeping an eye on the place and really learn its layout. More importantly, we'll see what them nasty folks down there all do with their time. Maybe we can slip into their routine."

"Then what?" Wildon asked.

"Then tomorrow night, we ride in and join the population," Garrity said. "If we're bold enough, maybe they'll think we're just a couple of the boys."

"Do you really think we could get away with that?" Wildon asked.

"We'd better," Garrity said. "Or we'll end up like them three fellers." He pointed down to the trio of men killed in the gunfight.

Other bandits were now dragging the corpses away.

CHAPTER 13

Second Lieutenant Wildon Boothe was so nervous with agitation and impatience that he could not keep still. He drummed his fingers on the rocks that hid him as he and Garrity slipped into the twelfth daylight hour of spying down into the desperados' settlement.

During all that time they had not had one sighting of Hester. Now Wildon's worst fears played actively through his mind. Had the callous brutes ravished and murdered her, leaving her body to mummify in the desert sun? Or was she being held in one of the crude huts down there as a plaything for numerous rough *bandidos*. Even as he lay there, she could be suffering humiliation and injury from their carnal desires. A hundred awful pictures swept through his mind, and each required a distinct, individual effort to fight it down.

"Sir!" Garrity whispered.

Glad to have something—anything—to occupy his mind, Wildon gratefully crawled over to the sergeant's observation point. "Yes?"

"I've been studying that place we picked to

sneak through," Garrity said. "When we first get in, we should slip into the shadows of those outlying adobe buildings there, see? Then we can easily move from there to any place we want to go. If anybody spots us, they'd just figger we wandered over from some other side of the settlement."

"Right," Wildon said. "Good idea. Are we going to bring our horses?"

Garrity shook his head. "Not this first time. We'd just have to sneak them out again."

Wildon was disappointed. "Then you don't figure we'll get her out right away, do you?"

"I'm sorry, sir."

Wildon sighed and checked the sun. "At any rate, we should be able to move in another half-hour."

"Yes, sir," Garrity said. Suddenly he uncharacteristically reached out and laid his hand on Wildon's shoulder. "I know this is rough on you. I'd like to say you're doing fine, young Lieutenant. I'm proud of you."

Wildon, genuinely pleased, smiled. "Thank you, Sergeant Garrity." The words from an older man he respected and admired made him feel better somehow as he settled back to continue the long period of observation.

That night was cloudier than the previous one, and when the sun finally disappeared over the far rim of the Santo Domingos, Wildon and Garrity had to walk with care to avoid falling. But the conditions made it easier to slip between the boulders and step out into the shadows of the nearest buildings.

Garrity took a deep breath. "Well, let's go."

Wildon nodded. "And let's forget the military courtesy."

They strolled boldly out into the light and wandered toward some thatched huts. Making a slow turn, they began a careful walk straight into the settlement's main avenue. Nervous and ready for any overt act of violence against them, the pair of interlopers relaxed when they drew but quick, casual glances from the people of the town.

The soldiers' eyes moved ceaselessly, taking in every detail possible. Each time they passed a building, they chanced quick looks inside to see if Hester was visible. But all they saw were rough-looking men and their women, eating and drinking in the early evening.

"I've noticed that ever'body here ain't a bandit," Garrity said. "Look there. An open-air gunsmithy is set up and there's an old lady selling tacos."

"What are tacos?" Wildon asked.

"Good food," Garrity said. "C'mon, Wildon."

"You bet, Jim," Wildon said.

Garrity bargained with the cook and finally procured a couple of chicken tacos for ten cents American. Wildon took a bite of the chicken-stuffed fried tortilla. "Good!"

Garrity tried his. "Sure is. Them Mexicans got

136

two good things going for them—their women and their food. If I ever marry, it's gonna be to a *mexicana*." He lowered his voice. "Anyhow we'll look better strolling around, munching tacos. I don't think these jaspers would figger a coupla spies would drop by for supper."

Wildon nodded. After they turned down another street, he spotted a sign. "I don't know Spanish, but even I can figure that's a good place to pay a visit." He pointed to an establishment identified as *La Cantina Americana*.

"Let's have a look," Garrity said.

Without increasing their pace, the pair of soldiers walked toward the crudely constructed saloon. It was a large adobe-walled structure with a tiled roof. The front was wide open, giving an excellent view into the interior where tables and chairs of different styles were arranged haphazardly around the place. A small bar, tended by a portly barkeep with a huge handlebar mustache, was situated along the center of the far wall.

It wasn't difficult to tell how the place got its name. All the customers were Americans. The only Mexicans were the staff. Wildon and Garrity chose a table near the bar and sat down. A comely waitress took their order for a couple of beers. She served them, then wandered off to tend the tables.

"How you boys doin'?"

Wildon glanced over and noticed a heavy-lidded

137

American at the next table. The lieutenant nodded. "We're fine, thank you."

The American raised his glass. "The more of us the better. When did you boys git in?"

"Just today," Garrity interjected. "We're just looking around."

"Y'all missed a job," the American said. "But it didn't amount to nothin'. An army wagon train with nothin' worth stealin'—and nothin' worth dyin' for."

Wildon took a sip of his beer, deciding to lead the conversation. "Nobody got a thing, huh?"

"Nope." Then the man laughed. " 'cept the boss. He got hisself a woman."

Garrity put his hand on Wildon's arm as a subtle hint to back off. "Well, that prob'ly didn't last long."

"Well, I don't know," the American drawled. "He took her to that there *castillo*."

"What castle?" Garrity answered.

A feminine voice behind him answered, "The big building in the *centro*." She smiled when the two soldiers looked at her. "Hello. I am called Lola."

"I'm Jim," Garrity said. "And this is Wildon. We just got in today."

"Pretty interesting about that woman," Wildon said, fighting to keep control.

Lola carefully looked at him. "It is nothing new for a bandit to take a woman for his own." She shrugged. "Most of the *mujeres* in this town were

138

stolen from someplace. They can't go back 'cause ever'body in their home village will look at them like *putas*—whores, you know?"

Garrity was getting worried about Wildon. He quickly downed his beer. "We'd best get along now."

Wildon took the hint. "Yeah," he said sullenly.

They wandered out of the bar and down the street. Wildon walked silently, looking up toward the big building in the middle of the settlement. His stomach churned with the knowledge that Hester was inside someplace.

They reached an alleyway of sorts. "Down here," Garrity said. He pulled the lieutenant into the shadows. "We're going back now. We know what to look for tomorrow."

They hurried behind the buildings. When they reached the *Cantina Americana,* there was a movement in the darkness. Then the fat bartender stepped out. But he wasn't offering any beer. Instead he held a Remington shotgun on them. He was quickly followed by Lola. The angry beauty of her face could be seen from the lantern light cast from the rear window.

"You are not *bandidos,*" Lola said. "You are here to find the *gringa!*"

"Just a minute, lady!" Garrity said alarmed. "You got us wrong."

"If you lie to me, I tell Jorge to kill you," Lola said.

139

Jorge the bartender exhibited a determined, silent sneer as he raised the double barrels.

Julio Montenegro's eyes were closed as he gently wafted the "Blue Danube Waltz" from his violin. Hester, remembering it was the first song that she and Wildon danced to at Fort MacNeil, could not smother her sentimental thoughts. She fought back the tears, but they trickled from her eyes.

Hubert Mauveaux, sitting across from her at the table, sighed aloud. "Ah, *ma chèrie* Camille! The beautiful song has touched your heart."

Hester's temper flared. "My name is not Camille! It is Mrs. Wildon Boothe. How many times must I tell you?"

"But Camille," Mauveaux said, "it would be so unromantic to say to you, 'I adore your beauty, Mrs. Wildon Boothe.'"

"You should not speak to me that way, *monsieur*," Hester insisted. "It is not proper."

"Why shouldn't I?" Mauveaux said, smiling in a cocky manner. "Did you not fight over me with the fiery Lola?"

"She attacked me!" Hester protested.

"That is not what *Señora* Gonzales told me," Mauveaux said. "She said you two were like *tigritas* in your feminine fury."

"I don't care what that old lady said," Hester cried out. She suddenly realized her protests might

140

be easily misinterpreted by the megalomaniac sitting at the dining table with her. She calmed down, deciding to use the Mexican woman to her personal advantage. "Lola loves you, *monsieur.* Call her to your side and reward her faithfulness. Marry her. For the love of God, marry her!"

"I cannot, for she does not have my heart," Mauveaux said. He snapped his fingers as a signal to Julio.

The violinist immediately changed his tune to Tchaikovsky's "Francesca da Rimini."

Mauveaux reached inside his uniform and produced a small velvet box. He slid it across the table. "Open it."

"I most certainly will not!"

He laughed. "Your teasing is so tantalizing, Camille." He took the box and opened it himself. Inside was a gold ring with a single, large pearl mounted in it. "To seal our pact of love, *ma chèrie!*"

A sudden idea leaped into Hester's mind. She damned herself for not thinking of it sooner. "Wait, *monsieur!*" Hester jumped up and ran into the next room where the bathtub still sat. She quickly returned with the soap clutched in her hand. "*Regardez!*" she cried out, tossing it on the table.

"Ah," he said with an unmistakable tone of relief in his voice. "You are going to bathe, *non?*"

"No! Look at that soap!"

141

Mauveaux, puzzled, shrugged. *"À quoi ça sert-il?"* he asked.

"It is Bristol soap, *monsieur,*" Hester said. "It is manufactured by my family."

"Your maiden name is Bristol?" he asked.

"I, sir, am Hester Bristol Boothe of Lake Champlain, New York," she said proudly.

"Hester!" he cried out. "Your name is Hester!"

"Oh, God!" Hester moaned.

"It is more lovely than Camille," Mauveaux proclaimed.

"You are missing the point, sir," Hester insisted. "My family will pay you handsomely to release me. All you have to do is have me delivered to my husband."

"I cannot give you up for money," Mauveaux exclaimed. "I am too much in love with you." He got up and walked around the table.

"Stay away from me!" Hester demanded as she fled to the other side.

Julio continued to play his violin rather absent-mindedly as he watched the drama being carried out before his eyes.

Mauveaux continued the chase, forcing Hester to flee around the table several times. The Frenchman was not discouraged. "We call this *la chasse,* no? Very well then, my lovely Hester. I am *le chasseur d'amour!"*

Hester's fury mounted. She began to find Julio's playing irritating. Finally, the next time she scurried to the other side of the table, the angry young woman grabbed the man's violin and spun around. When Mauveaux approached, she brought it crashing down on his head.

The Frenchman staggered back, bruised but happy. *"Mon dieu!"* he cried out. "I believe you would be a tigress in leather!"

"Keep the hands high!" Lola warned Wildon and Garrity. "If at anytime I don't see them, I tell Jorge to shoot. One shot kill you both from the scattergun, hey?"

"Seguro," Garrity agreed in Spanish. "Don't let Jorge get too excited now. There's no reason for it."

Jorge emphasized his perfect understanding of the situation by swinging the barrels back and forth a bit. "I kill you, *gringos,"* he said.

"Not to worry, sir and madam," Wildon said in a soothing voice. "I believe this can all be sorted out."

"I know you came to look for the *gringa* that Movo came back with," Lola said.

"No, *señorita,"* Garrity said, vigorously shaking his head remembering that the girl in the farming village had identified the bandit chief as Movo. "We are—"

"Silencio!" she hissed. "Do you think I am an *estupida?"*

Wildon decided it was time for candor. "We can make a deal with you. If you don't turn us in, we can make it well worth your while, madam."

Lola laughed. "You don't understand, *gringo*. I want you to take her away."

"I beg your pardon," Wildon said, not quite believing he had heard the words.

"I don't like that *americana,* see? Movo is *mi hombre*—my man," Lola said. "He is wild about her. So much so that he has not even touched her."

Wildon's eyes opened wide in happy surprise. "Really?"

"I know it for the truth," Lola said. "The old woman who works there has told me this."

Wildon sighed with relief. "I shall guarantee you our most enthusiastic cooperation."

"He means we'll do our best to get her away," Garrity said. He pointed to Jorge. "Don't think he could put that thing away now?"

"Sure," Lola said. She nodded to her bartender. "*Abaja la escopeta.*" When he had obeyed, she turned back to the two soldiers. "I tell you the truth, I want to kill her. I want to scratch out her eyes. But to do so would only make Humberto hate me. I could not stand that. But if she goes away, he will forget and love me again."

"You're certainly right about that," Wildon said enthusiastically.

"Where is she being kept?" Garrity asked.

"In the big building there in the middle," Lola explained. "It is called *El Castillo*."

"We noticed it earlier," Wildon said. "It seems a well-guarded place. I believe it would be most difficult to break into."

"I can get you in there," Lola said. "But not tonight. I must make arrangements. Do you have horses?"

"Yes," Garrity said. "But only two. We need one for the young lady."

"I will get you one," Lola said. "Tomorrow night you come back here with your horses. Come to my cantina and wait. When the time is right, I will take you to *El Castillo*. We will go inside and get the girl. Then we come out, and you get on the horses and leave."

"After we leave with the *americana,* we will have to wait in our camp until daylight," Garrity pointed out. "It will be too dangerous to go down the mountain in the dark.

"They will find you," Lola said. "The best thing is to go straight to the front entrance and down the path. If you are bold and act like you belong here, the guards will not bother you."

"It is risky," Wildon protested.

Lola laughed sarcastically. "Jorge will be nearby, *señores*. If you fail or falter, he will kill you. I do not want you to become prisoners and betray me to my beloved Humberto."

"Looks like we're damned if we do and damned

if we don't," Wildon said.

"That is absolutely *correcto*," Lola replied. She waved them away. *"Hasta mañana en la noche —* until tomorrow night."

CHAPTER 14

Wildon Boothe had never been a patient person. Adulthood had done nothing to curb the disquiet he had as a youngster. In those days he had always been impetuous and anxious for any sort of physical action. He would spend sleepless nights in anticipation of the next day's hunting or horseback-riding excursion. Now, with Hester's rescue close at hand, every nerve in his body seemed to be in a screaming state of alertness.

Garrity, calmly smoking his pipe as he leaned up against his saddle, thought it best to keep the officer's mind occupied. "At least one problem is took care of, sir."

Wildon, nervously scratching nonsensical designs in the dirt, looked over at the sergeant. "What sort of problem?"

Garrity pointed to the horses and saddles. "If we couldn't bring them back with us, we'd be in a lot of trouble."

"You mean if we had to steal bandit horses for the escape?"

"Yes, sir," Garrity said. "If we abandoned our mounts, it would be a loss of government property."

"I wouldn't give a damn," Wildon said.

"You'd still have to write a report," Garrity pointed out. "Sergeant Mulvaney would be fit to be tied when we showed up without the stuff we left with."

"Even if we sacrificed it to rescue my wife?"

"That wouldn't make any difference according to the regulations," Garrity said.

"God damn the regulations then," Wildon said. "But you're right. They'd probably have taken it out of my pay."

"That's for sure. And you'd probably never get a promotion. You'd end up being the oldest second lieutenant in the history of the United States Army."

"Wouldn't that be a hell of a note?" Wildon remarked.

Garrity finished his pipe and knocked it against a rock to get the ashes out. "As it is, you're going to have to write one hell of a report to explain why you left your command in the middle of an official transfer."

"Believe it or not, I've given some thought to that between worrying about Hester," Wildon said. "I think I can justify it though."

"It'd be a pretty cold-blooded board of officers that would give you a hard time over that," Garrity agreed. He stuck his pipe in his jacket pocket. "We really should give more thought to that Mexican woman."

"Lola?" Wildon asked. "What do you have on your mind?"

"I'm hoping like hell we can really trust her," Garrity said.

"Sure we can, Sergeant," Wildon said. "I believe her when she says she wants us to get Hester away from there. If she wants to marry that man, she'd do whatever necessary to get rid of any competition."

"Maybe," Garrity mused. "But she would still accomplish her aim if the three of us were gunned down."

"I don't think so," Wildon said. "Remember the woman told us that the bandit chief would never forgive her if she killed Hester."

"If *she* killed her," Garrity said. "But what if that goddamned Jorge cut loose on us with the scattergun? Lola would be in the clear and her barkeep could claim he was just shooting up some outsiders without knowing the woman was there."

Wildon was thoughtful. "That takes some of the brightness out of the picture, doesn't it?"

"This thing has been chancy from the start," Garrity said. "We shouldn't let our guard down just because we've been offered some help."

"Then I say we go in and out of there expecting the worse," Wildon said.

"I'm all for that," Garrity replied. With that bit of business settled, the sergeant yawned. "This seems like a good time for a nap."

Wildon stood up. "Sleep is out of the question for me. Maybe I'll go for a walk."

"It'd be better if you walked *down* instead of *up* the mountain, sir," Garrity pointed out. "There wouldn't be as big a chance of being spotted."

"As usual, Sergeant Garrity, your advice is sound," Wildon said. "I'll stroll down the slope a bit. Maybe it'll take away some of the tension, and I can get some sleep before tonight's action."

"I'll see you later, sir." Garrity rolled over and placed his hat over his head to shield him from the sun.

Wildon walked slowly and thoughtfully, picking his way carefully as he left the camp. He stopped and stared out over the panorama that spread out from where he stood on the mountain.

The terrain's appearance was alien to the native New Yorker. Bare, sun-baked boulders swept downward from the top of Bandido Mountain to the desert floor below. From that point on, the land was as flat and featureless as a table top. Smooth and unsullied, the badlands rolled on undisturbed to the far horizon. Wildon had never appreciated distances in the past, but it was breathtaking to consider the hundreds of square miles that were visible to the naked eye.

The scene, rather than making him feel insignificant with the awesome display of natural magnificence, gave him a feeling of power. Manly pride crept into the young cavalry officer. With the thought of rescuing his wife from bandits that night heavy on his mind, he felt aggressive and anxious to fight. He looked out over the endless landscape.

"This is my land," he said softly to himself, "and I was put on this earth to conquer it and call it a part of my own people's domain." He felt like an officer of an ancient Roman legion bringing civilization into the land of the Goths.

He resumed his walk, treading easily across the rocks as he descended another hundred feet. Breathing deeply and moving with restless energy, his steps were measured and regular despite the rugged terrain.

The Indian dove on him from behind, coming out of a hidden crop of boulders.

Both men crashed to the ground. Instinctively angry, Wildon kicked out and got to his feet. His opponent had done the same. Without hesitating, the Indian launched another attack. It was then that Wildon noticed the knife in the man's hand. When the attacker lunged with it, Wildon locked his hand on the man's wrist, reaching for his pistol. But the Indian now held the white man's wrist.

They struggled against each other, grunting and pulling, each trying to bring the other down. Dust flew up as they kicked and scuffled. Their whirling battle reached the edge of a slight ledge and they fell off, once again rolling and grappling.

The Indian was husky and short, with heavy muscles in his shoulders and upper arms. Although Wildon was much slimmer and lighter, his fury gave him extra strength. The fight was nip and tuck, but finally Wildon's lesser physical abilities began to allow the other an advantage. The attacker pushed and pressed with all the power in his body, until he finally pinned the white man down.

Wildon struggled, but eventually he could feel the knife edge across the top of his forehead. Then he realized the Indian meant to scalp him alive. He frantically renewed his struggling, but his opponent maintained his advantage, pressing the knife into his skin.

Suddenly the Indian's eyes opened wide and blood gushed from his mouth. His muscles relaxed a bit and Wildon kicked him off. He scrambled back and saw Garrity calmly pulling his knife from the man's back.

"Hell of a fight, sir," Garrity said. He rolled the man over and cut his throat with a deep gash, causing blood to spurt out and run down the rocks. "That's a goddamned Yaqui," he said stepping back to inspect his handiwork.

Wildon stood up, feeling shaky. "Do you think he was a part of the bandit gang?"

"No," Garrity answered. "Them Injuns don't do nothing 'cept with their own kind. He's part of a hunting group or a war party that must've wandered in through here."

Now Wildon drew his pistol. "You mean there're more than just this one devil?"

"Damn right," Garrity said. "And we'd better get outta here."

Wildon looked back at the Yaqui. The Indian's head was set at a strange angle due to the deep cut across his throat. "What the hell did he attack me for?"

"Hell, sir, he didn't need no reason," Garrity said. "The sonofabitch just likes to kill people."

"This is a cruel land," Wildon said, suddenly not feeling quite so sure of himself.

"That's why men like us is out here, sir," Garrity said. "Leading thirteen-dollar-a-month cavalry troopers to tame it."

Wildon looked again at the mutilated cadaver, the eyes open wide as they still displayed savage rage. "That is a mean son of a bitch," the lieutenant said.

"Sir," Garrity replied. "He is probably the meanest sonofabitch you're ever gonna meet."

"Then I got that over early in life, didn't I?" Wildon said. "By the way—thanks a hell of a lot."

"Don't mention it, sir," Garrity said.

"Well, let's get back up into camp and rest up

153

for tonight."

The Santo Domingo Mountains were cloaked in inky blackness. Only the occasional flashes of lamps or fires from various huts where people were staying up late lit the bandit town.

Garrity stepped out into the open from the boulders. He took a quick look in all directions, then signaled Wildon to follow. The officer, leading their mounts, walked into the camp, handing over Garrity's reins to the sergeant. Wordlessly and with forced nonchalance, they strolled between the ramshackle buildings until they reached the back of the *Cantina Americana*. They saw another horse, saddled and ready, already tied up there.

Wildon rapped lightly on the door. It was opened by a young woman he recognized as one of the barmaids. She beckoned him and Garrity to enter.

Lola, drinking coffee and counting her receipts for the evening, glanced over at them. *"Momento,"* she said.,

Jorge the bartender, without the shotgun but wearing a pistol, looked dully over at the two Americans.

When Lola finished, she put the money in a small strongbox. Jorge walked over and picked up the heavy item, walking out the back with it.

Lola put a shawl over her shoulders. "You are ready?"

"I was wondering if that bandit chief Movo would be there," Garrity said.

"Sure," Lola said. "He took a woman to bed with him."

Garrity grinned. "You sure got problems with your man's faithfulness, don't you?"

"Hey! He don't love her," Lola protested. "What do I care, eh?" She looked at Wildon. "You better don't forget he loves your wife. Want to go now?"

"Yes," Wildon said impatiently.

"Then let us go," Lola said. She picked up a sombrero and serape off the table where she had been working, and walked out the door with the barmaid following.

"Wait a minute," Garrity said, pointing to the younger woman. "What's she coming along for?"

"There is a reason, *gringo,*" Lola said. "You will see."

The four people skirted around the back way of the town. Keeping to the deep shadows, they walked behind the various huts and shacks until they reached a point that looked directly at the bandit chief's large structure.

Lola looked carefully around. She snapped her fingers and the barmaid scurried up to her. Lola pointed to the guard in front of the Castle. *"Andale!"*

The girl pulled her blouse off her shoulders and down far enough to expose a tantalizing glimpse of her breasts. Walking seductively, she boldly crossed the open space and walked up to the guard. She and the man spoke for a few brief moments. Finally, after looking carefully around, the two walked quickly away from the door to the other side of the building.

"Now we go," Lola said.

The trio quickly approached the *Castillo,* going up to the entrance. Lola pulled a large key from her skirt and carefully inserted it, turning it slowly until a click sounded. She pushed the portal open, leading them into the foyer and to a staircase.

A light from a lamp suddenly came on from a room off to one side. Lola pushed Wildon and Garrity to the other side of the stairs.

"Quien esta?" came *Señora* Gonzalez' voice.

Lola went to her door. *"Soy yo Lola."*

The old woman mumbled something but turned her lamp off. Lola beckoned to the two cavalrymen. They followed her up to the second floor. After going into another room, Lola grabbed Wildon's arm. "She is in there."

Wildon, walking rapidly but carefully, went to the door on the far side of the chamber. He opened it and stepped in. "Hester darling?" he called out in a loud whisper. "Hester!"

There was a rustle on the bed. A figure sat up.

"Who is there?"

Wildon rushed over. "Dearest! It's me. Wildon."

"Darling!" she cried out.

"Shhh!" he cautioned her.

Hester slid off the bed and rushed to his arms. They embraced tightly, kissing each other's face over and over before settling down to one long buss on the mouth. When they parted, she reached out and felt his face. "Oh, dearest Wildon! I knew you would come."

"Are you all right, my love?" Wildon asked.

"Yes! Yes! Now that you are here," Hester said. "Oh, sweet Lord, Wildon!"

"We have to be fast, darling," Wildon said. "We've planned this out. Three horses are waiting for us."

"Three?"

"Yes. Sergeant Garrity came with me," Wildon explained.

"Bless his brave heart," Hester said. "And yours too."

"Now you must be quiet, darling. It is very dangerous."

The two went into the next room. Lola, without ceremony, handed over the sombrero and serape. "Wear these, *gringa*," she said. "And keep the hat tipped low, eh? We don't want nobody to see who you are."

"What is she doing here?" Hester asked coldly.

"I'll explain later, dearest," Wildon said. "Please

157

put the things on."

Hester quickly slipped the serape over her shoulders and set the sombrero on her head. She noticed Garrity standing to one side. "Hello, Sergeant Garrity."

"How are you, Mrs. Boothe?"

"I'm —"

Lola hissed at them. "Are you going to talk all night or get out of here?"

The Mexican woman turned to the door and led them back down the stairs. After being extra careful when they passed *Señora* Gonzalez' room, the group eased back outside. Once there, they moved back into the darkness.

Garrity pulled his pistol and tapped Wildon's shoulder. "Watch out for Jorge, sir."

"Right," Wildon said. He put one arm around Hester while holding the Remington in his free hand.

But when they reached the back of the cantina, the only living creatures were the three horses. Lola pointed to the animals. "Now! *Larganse* — get out of here!"

They got into the saddles. After Wildon reached over and pulled Hester's sombrero even lower, they allowed the mounts to walk slowly over toward the main entrance. A bright lantern burned where the two guards sleepily stood their posts. As they drew closer, Hester suddenly stiffened.

"What's the matter?" Wildon asked.

"One of those men knows me," Hester said. "He plays the violin."

"Violin? What in the—"

"Never mind," Garrity interrupted. "Keep your hat down low, Mrs. Boothe."

They continued to approach the guards. Both bandits looked over at them, displaying no special sign of recognition. The three drew closer until they were within fifteen yards of the exit—then ten yards—and finally five yards.

The sentries, bored, sleepy, and tired, showed no interest. After a cursory glance, they simply looked the other way. Wildon, Hester, and Garrity rode into the lantern light and turned toward the path that would lead down Bandido Mountain.

A man, on foot and limping badly up the trail toward them, suddenly came into view in the pale illumination. He looked at Wildon and Garrity, then shouted, *"Alto! Alto! Son soldados americanos!"*

It was the bandit they had accosted earlier with the lame horse.

CHAPTER 15

Wildon swung up the barrel of the Winchester and pulled the trigger in a coldly calculated but instantaneous act. The bullet hit the bandit in the chest, lifting him up off his feet and flinging him straight onto his back.

Garrity's pistol barked three times. The first bullet went into Julio Montenegro's abdomen, folding him over before he twisted to one side and hit the ground. His violin-playing days ended as he rolled onto his stomach to die. His companion, sleepy and slow, also went down. Two of Garrity's bullets had torn him up inside. He slumped to his knees, then pitched face forward into the dirt.

"Ride out!" Wildon said to Hester.

She was already slapping the reins and kicking the horse's flanks when her husband spoke. Now the two men followed, wasting no time in beginning the run for freedom. The echoes of the gunplay still sounded through the mountain passes as they thundered down the long trail to the desert below.

Up in the bandit camp, the more sober inhabitants were awakened by the shots. Most sighed in minor irritation, rolling over to go back to sleep. Others, more curious about who had shot whom, came out of their quarters. The fight had been so abrupt and lasted such a short time that no one knew exactly what had happened. Most milled around a bit, thinking that a violent argument, so common in their group, had broken out and was now settled. Nothing to become excited about. The bodies could always be buried the next day.

Up in his room, Hubert Mauveaux sat up in bed. He slapped the buttocks of the wench beside him. "Go to the window and see what's going on."

The woman slipped from the covers and padded over to look outside. "There was a fight by the *entrada*," she said. "There are three men dead."

Mauveaux was thoughtful for a few moments. "What could have happened to cause a fracas there?" He joined the woman at the window. He could see one of his senior lieutenants below. "*Oye,* Paco! What has happened there?"

Paco Fuentes looked up at the window in *El Castillo*. "I don't know, *mi general*. I was getting ready for bed when I heard the shots. Then some riders headed down the trail. It seemed like somebody fought their way through the guards. *Porque?*"

"I don't know why," Mauveaux said. "We have

161

no prisoners locked in the *carcel*. So who—" He stopped speaking in mid-sentence as his eyes widened. He turned from the window and rushed from the room. Running down the hall, he burst into the dining room and hurried to the door. He opened it and looked at the bed where Hester Boothe slept.

"Vide," he said in French. "She has been taken away." The bandit chief ran to the nearest window. "Paco! Paco!"

Fuentes had started back to his hut, but he quickly responded to his chief's call. *"Si, mi general?"*

"Call out our best men," Mauveaux shouted. "Someone has taken my woman."

"Immediatemente!" Fuentes, knowing the importance of such an event to Mauveaux, rushed to obey.

The moonlight was erratic because of the clouds. Moments of good visibility offered only the barest minimum of glimpses at the trail before it quickly grew dark again. Garrity fully realized the peril of continuing the ride at the rapid pace they were maintaining.

"Lieutenant! Lieutenant!" he called out. "Hold it up!"

Wildon, a few paces ahead of Hester, pulled in on his reins and moved his horse over to force hers to slow down. When they stopped, he turned and waited for Garrity. He was irritated by this halt in the escape. "Yes, Sergeant?"

"We can't keep riding this fast, sir," Garrity said. "Or we're gonna take a wrong step and go off the trail."

"I've been thinking about that too, but I was in too much of a hurry to consider slowing down," Wildon admitted, glancing over at the empty blackness. "It's hundreds of feet to the desert floor. But if we slacken our pace too much, the bandits will catch up with us."

"Yes, sir. I figger they're getting ready to come after us now. We got to hit that desert with enough time to outdistance 'em."

"The only obvious answer is a rear-guard action," Wildon said, pulling his Winchester from its boot. "You are to escort my wife back to the baggage train, Sergeant. I'll hold them off as long as I can."

Garrity shook his head. "Your missus needs you more'n me, sir. I'll do it."

"No, Sergeant," Wildon said. "It's my duty. Get her back to our people."

Garrity leaned forward in the saddle. "You listen to me, young Lieutenant. This is one order you ain't giving. I'm in command right now. I'll stay here and delay the pursuit. Then I can cut loose and catch up with you. By then you ought to be out in the desert."

163

"Just a goddamned minute!" Wildon protested.

"Be logical, sir. Your wife isn't going to leave you here. I can travel a hell of a lot faster than you two and I can rejoin you. If I don't make it, it's soljer's luck. If you didn't make it, I'd have to face your missus." He grinned. "Frankly I'd rather go gun-on-gun with ever' bandit up on Bandido Mountain."

"I can't say I blame you," Wildon said.

Hester interrupted. "Will you two stop talking about me as if I were someplace else? And Sergeant Garrity is absolutely right, darling. I will not leave without you."

"That's that, sir," Garrity said. "Ride!"

"Yes, Sergeant. I'll expect you to catch up with us on the desert."

"Count on it, sir," Garrity replied.

Wildon turned and, with Hester at his side, set off down the trail at as fast a pace as safety allowed.

Garrity waited until they were completely out of sight. He took his horse farther below and found a place to tie him to a manzanita branch. When the animal was secure, the sergeant went upward and found a good fighting position within the rocks. He made sure the Henry rifle was fully loaded, and set a few loose rounds in front of him.

Then he settled down to wait.

Ten minutes passed in silence. The moon eased

164

past the clouds and cast its bright yellow light over the scene. Garrity could see the trail upward for fifty yards. He picked a spot where the bandits would first appear.

It was a quarter of an hour later when Garrity heard the approaching hooves. He picked up the Henry and waited. The shadows of the riders appeared at a higher level on the trail. The sergeant waited until the first man reached the point he had chosen.

The shot blasted out, rolling the rider over the rump of his horse. The second shot emptied another bandit saddle, and the third brought down a horse. A warbling, fading scream showed the rider had been pitched over the side of the trail.

Garrity worked the lever of the rifle. He coolly recalled a similar incident on a backwoods Virginia road in '64 as he listened to the sounds of men bringing their animals to quick stops. He could see a crowd of them ganging up on the trail. The sergeant didn't take time to aim. He pointed the barrel at the small mob and let the Henry blast away.

Shouts and curses sounded along with two thuds as a pair of the desperados fell to the ground. The survivors rode back in a spontaneous move.

Garrity took advantage of the lull to shove some more rounds into his weapon. He licked his dry lips and reached for the canteen he had slung over his shoulder. The water was still cool and sweet. Tomorrow on the desert it would be warm and stale.

If he were alive to drink it.

An abrupt thundering of hooves sounded above. Garrity knew what they were trying to do. They would make a wild rush, hoping to overpower the ambush site. Prepared and determined, he waited as he carefully watched his chosen aiming point. When the first man reached it, the Henry belched fire and slugs again.

The first man was blown sideways from the saddle, hitting the rocks and the inside of the trail when he fell off. The bandit immediately behind him bumped into his friend's hesitant horse. That made his own mount veer and he rode straight off the trail into empty sky. Both he and his stallion silently sailed downward to be crushed on the rocks below.

Garrity missed the third man, but he picked up the fourth and took him out with a head shot. Then he turned his attention back to the third who was now pounding closer. The sergeant pulled his revolver from his holster and fired two times. The man slipped off and bounced on the trail twice before coming to a stop. His horse continued galloping toward the bottom of the mountain.

Getting very serious, Garrity fired methodically. He picked each target, took careful aim, and shot each man. He was almost rhythmic about it as he performed the action eight times to hit as many bandits.

Now it was silent except for the whining breeze.

Garrity knew the bandits had pulled back. Not knowing what they faced, there was no doubt they would slow down their attempts and make a time-consuming sneak attack against his position.

But the sergeant wasn't planning on sticking around.

Keeping to the shadows, he eased back to his horse. Garrity led the animal for fifty yards down the mountain track before he mounted up. Then he rode down the trail toward the desert to link up with Lieutenant Boothe and his wife.

Garrity had gone a bit over two hundred yards when he heard the shots ahead. Going for his pistol again, he drew the revolver and slowed down his horse. When he came around a bend, he saw Hester Boothe behind a large boulder holding onto two horses.

"Mrs. Boothe!"

She turned and looked back at him. "Thank God you've come, Sergeant Garrity."

He was puzzled and worried. "What's going on, ma'am? You should've been down in the desert by now."

"We almost stumbled straight into some guards on the trail," Hester explained. "Wildon has been trading shots with the rascals."

"Well, ma'am," Garrity said. "Here's one more horse for you to take care of." He handed her the reins and crept forward. He finally spotted Wildon behind some rocks. "Lieutenant! It's me," he said to announce himself and avoid accidentally getting shot. "I'm coming down there."

"Come ahead, Sergeant," Wildon Boothe shouted back.

Garrity made his way through the rocks. A bullet struck close by his head, ricocheting off into the night. "Goddamn!" he panted. He took a deep breath, then sprinted forward to fling himself down beside the lieutenant. "How're you doing, sir? Can you see 'em good?"

"There're two of them," Wildon said. "In a little natural fort about twenty yards ahead. I couldn't get past them." He raised up slightly and fired a shot. He ducked back down. "How'd you do?"

"Fine, sir. The bastards is holed up right now, but when they figger I'm gone, they're gonna come hell-for-leather down that trail."

"In other words, we must get out of here," Wildon said.

"Them's the *exact* words, sir, and we ain't got a whole lot of time," Garrity said. He raised his head for a quick look, then stooped back behind the rock.

"I think it's time for fire-and-maneuver, Sergeant," Wildon said. "It looks like we can go

168

wide left and right and keep them in the middle. If we cover each other, it shouldn't take more than ten minutes."

"Let's make it five, sir," Garrity said. He pulled his pistol again. "I'll go right. Cover me, sir."

Wildon once again raised up. He fired rapidly while Garrity ran to other cover farther ahead. When the sergeant reached the point, he began a rapid fusillade.

Now Wildon made his move. He veered off left and ran as fast as he could. After diving behind some rocks, he came up shooting.

Garrity took advantage of his turn to gain some higher ground. When he reached the point, he could see a couple of more good firing sites to move to.

Bruised and scratched from diving into a pile of rocks, Wildon didn't notice the pain as he raced toward a stand of manzanita growing beside a large slab of rock. When he arrived, the lieutenant was able to cut loose with another volley before he had to reload.

By that time Garrity was again on the move.

The action was repeated three more times. The pair of bandit guards had grown confused by the tactics. The first indication they were in serious trouble was when some shots from their left hit one of them. He slumped to the ground. His friend unwisely but instinctively pulled back from the direction of attack.

And stumbled straight into Wildon's line of fire.

Wildon unemotionally and intentionally aimed at the bandit. A gentle squeeze on the trigger and he killed the man. He turned and emitted a loud whistle. "Hester! Bring the horses!"

In five minutes the trio of escapees were remounted and going down the trail. When they reached the bottom, they streaked out over the hard desert floor, heading with all speed back to safety. The sun, a bare reddish disk, was just peeking over the eastern horizon.

Above them, on the trail he now knew was clear, Hubert Mauveaux led his bandits down the trail at a wild gallop.

CHAPTER 16

The previous night's coolness had yet to be burned away by the desert's relentless sun. The comfortable temperature acted as a stimulant to the horses as Wildon, Hester, and Garrity streaked across the hard-baked terrain.

Hester rode between the two men, sitting in the saddle and rocking in rhythm with each stride of her mount in a smooth fashion. She was completely at ease and even enjoying the ride, showing what a superb horsewoman she truly was.

Wildon glanced back and noted that there was no sign of the bandits in pursuit. The three escapees' mounts would tire fast at that frantic pace, but they had no choice. If they slowed up to take it easy on the animals, it would only increase the danger of being overtaken. All three knew that the desperados would be pushing hard to catch up with them.

Another ten minutes of the mad galloping continued. Garrity's eyes were in constant motion as he checked the area in front of them, the condition of his companions and their animals, and any sightings of the outlaws. He saw nothing to give him any concern other than the very real potential of sure death they faced if they were captured by the bandits. But he did notice that Hester's horse was not as fit or fleet as the cavalry mounts he and the young lieutenant rode.

Wildon had also become aware of that particular problem. Although the animal Hester rode was game and showed every desire to keep up with his new companions, he was slowly falling behind. Wildon looked back again to see if the *bandidos* were any closer. When he noted they were not, he emitted a loud whistle to catch the others' attention. When they looked toward him he signaled a halt.

The horses, excited by the run, whinnied protests as the reins were pulled back against them. They finally slowed, kicking up dust, then came to a hoof-stomping, snorting stop, showing their equine displeasure at the interruption of what they considered fun.

"What's up, sir?" Garrity asked.

"I'm going to trade horses with Hester," Wildon answered, swinging out of the saddle.

"Sir—"

"By God, Sergeant Garrity, I'll tolerate no arguing this time," Wildon said angrily. He looked up at Hester. "Let's exchange mounts."

Hester, with a solid background in judging

horses, knew the reason. She would have preferred that Garrity take her mount, but something about the way Wildon looked smothered any desire for argument. She stepped to the ground without a word.

Now Wildon settled into the saddle of the bandit horse. After waiting for Hester to remount his own animal, he glanced toward the rear. A faint cloud of dust could easily be seen hanging just on the horizon.

"See that, Sergeant Garrity?" Wildon asked. "They're drawing closer."

"They sure are, sir," Garrity said. "Let's ride."

The run for freedom was resumed.

Forced to push the horses again, the trio galloped at a continuing mad pace. Wildon slapped the reins onto the horse's shoulders, but could sense the animal's fast-growing fatigue. Each stride set him back farther from the other two mounts.

Wildon looked back and saw that there was a perceptive change in the dust cloud. Higher, thick, and definitely closer, its ominous sight heralded the closing gap between them and the outlaws.

"Ha-yaah!" Wildon shouted, trying to urge the horse on. The animal tried, but still could not maintain the pace of the other two.

Finally Garrity rode out a bit farther ahead. Then he zigzagged back and forth to slow the married couple down and brought them to another halt. "You gotta gimme that horse, sir."

"I thought I made myself clear, Sergeant," Wildon said, pulling rank.

Hester rode over close to her husband. "Darling, do what you think is best. But I am telling you, without hesitation, that I shall stick close to your side."

"Will neither of you obey me as an officer or husband?" Wildon asked angrily.

"Now look, Lieutenant. You know your wife ain't gonna ride off and leave you," Garrity argued. "I thought you'd already seen that. If you keep riding that damned Mexican horse, you're both gonna be farther and farther behind. This way, you stand a better chance of getting away. Hell, I can prob'ly do pretty good for myself if I'm alone anyhow. At least I won't have nobody else to worry about if I get separated from you two."

"Perhaps we can pull another rear-guard action," Wildon suggested.

Garrity shook his head. "There's no cover. Even if one of us stayed behind, them bandits would just ride around and come back later after getting the other two."

Wildon took another look at the horizon. The dust cloud seemed to have grown in the previous few minutes. "Very well, Sergeant."

Within seconds, the two cavalrymen had exchanged mounts.

This time Wildon and Hester took the lead while Garrity brought up the rear on the blown bandit horse. They rode wildly with abandon, giving the eager animals their heads. Only Garrity's stallion strained in an effort to go all out.

They went up a slight rise and down into what appeared to be flatlands. Then the unexpected sights of arroyos appeared. A disorganized network of ancient riverbeds formed an erratic pattern of trenches ahead of them. Wildon and Hester urged their horses to jump the ravines. But when Garrity reached the gashes in the earth, he chose the widest and rode down into it, dismounting and pulling the Henry from its scabbard.

As with the ambush on the mountain trail, the sergeant had the luxury of preparing himself well in order to surprise his enemy. The disadvantage of this position was the fact that the bandits would not be pinned down to the confines of a narrow track. But the arroyos still offered a chance, albeit limited, of slowing them down.

Garrity took the time available to him to go to several different positions in the arroyo that offered good areas of fire. He chose the one that gave him the best view. It would be his main fighting post.

Its depth was a foot more than his height, but there were plenty of places that offered footholds so that he could step up into a firing position

175

and drop back under cover before any accurate return fire could be directed at him. When he finished the task of picking his spots, he went back to the one that was his first choice. Stepping up onto the bank, he cautiously raised his head until his eyes were at ground level. He could easily see the bandit gang approaching. The dark shadows in front of the dust were barely distinguishable, but Garrity knew dozens of riders thundered toward him.

This particular ambush would be carried out at maximum range. He had to wait a full five minutes before the *bandidos* reached the point where he planned to shoot. Aiming high to allow for the bullet's drop at that yardage, he pointed the muzzle at a point in front of the large, approaching target. He knew the desperados would not even hear the shot as he squeezed the trigger.

One of the horses suddenly went down, throwing its rider to the dirt while the rest of the gang pressed on.

Even though Garrity was but one man, he had every intention of hiding the fact from the bandits. He quickly went to another point and repeated the operation. After firing five more rounds, he stopped long enough to see what sort of reaction the outlaws had made to the unexpected casualties among themselves.

They were coming to a ragged halt, milling around and gesturing to each other. Laughing out loud, Garrity ran to his horse and leaped into the saddle. Thoroughly pleased with himself, the sergeant rode out of the arroyo and up onto level ground to gallop off after Wildon and Hester.

Wildon had glanced back and noticed Garrity turning off into the arroyo. He was torn between whether or not to go back to the sergeant and stand side by side with him in a shoot-out with the bandits. It was sorely tempting to the adventurous, soldiering side of the young lieutenant's soul. But a look at his wife swept away his warrior instinct, replacing it with that of a loving, dutiful husband.

Hester was also doing more than simply riding blindly toward freedom. She used her own eyes to judge the situation. When Garrity pulled away, she kept a close check on Wildon to see what he would do. Hester was determined that if her man pulled back, she would ride with him. When he continued the pace, she stuck close to his side.

It was Hester who noted Garrity when he rode out of the dry riverbeds. She motioned to Wildon. As if making a silent agreement between them, they slowed enough to allow the sergeant to rejoin them. When he caught up, the run continued.

Wildon, with a sense of direction and location developed through countless hunting trips in the Catskills, recognized they were near the Mexican farming village they had visited earlier. An idea formed in his mind.

"This way! This way!" he shouted as loud as he could. A slight tug on the reins turned his horse in the direction he wanted to go.

Garrity also recognized the terrain. As if in agreement, he unhesitatingly veered his own direction to go with Wildon. The three rode another ten minutes before the small adobe huts came into view.

When they reached the place, the three found the same kind of impromptu welcoming committee that had previously greeted Wildon and Garrity—the hamlet's men.

The spokesman, remembered by the two Americans as being the one who forsook his raped wife, exhibited no pleasure at seeing them. He gave Hester a meaningful glance. "You have found *la mujer americana,* eh?"

"Yes," Wildon said. "My wife."

"You are a lucky man, *señor,*" the Mexican said. "I do not understand why you do not race on to *la frontera.*"

The other village men crowded around ominously. They seemed to sense the situation the three Americans were in. The spokesman asked, "What do you want from us, *señores?*"

"We need *ayuda,*" Garrity explained. *"Los bandidos* chase us. We have to hide."

"There is no place for you to hide," the Mexican said. "Go away. You bring the bandits here."

He turned toward the crowd. "Luis! Alfredo! *Vengan con tus armas!*"

Two men pushed their way through the others. When they stepped out into the open, they each held a weapon—one a pistol and the other a rifle. Their manner showed they were ready and willing to shoot.

"If you do not go, I will tell them to kill you," the Mexican said.

"Wait," Wildon said. "We have not harmed you."

"But you bring such *daño* to us," the man said. "If the bandits come and find your tracks going away from here, they will quickly leave and follow you. *En cambio,* if they find your bodies, they will reward us."

Alarm swept through Wildon and Garrity. Both men, though neither spoke to the other, had sudden thoughts of drawing pistols and shooting.

The Mexican sighed. "But we are *cristianos* here. *Por eso* if you wish to leave, we will allow it."

The three escapees took the hint. "We will go then," Garrity said. He looked at Wildon and Hester. "There's no sense in wasting any more time. It'll only make things worse for us."

"Then let's go," Wildon said.

The three Americans quickly rode away without further word.

They realized they had lost even the small bit

of time gained through Garrity's ambush. They pressed on toward the border. But the sergeant's horse was faltering much more. Although a spirited animal, it was not capable of keeping up the run more than another three miles at best.

To make matters worse, the two cavalry mounts were beginning to show the physical strain they were under. Slowed considerably, the ride continued northward. Finally, when they reached the outer stretch of the arroyo patterns they had encountered earlier, Garrity spoke the obvious.

"Let's find a good spot. We ain't gonna make any more headway."

They continued for another half-mile before finding a deep cut in the desert floor. Riding down into it, they dismounted. Wildon and Garrity handed the reins over to Hester as they pulled their long guns from the saddle boots. The two climbed back up the bank to see if they could spot the bandits' approach.

"We're as good as being on foot," Garrity said. "And that's a fact whether we like it or not."

"Yes," Wildon said. "Now the army mounts are winded. The bandit horses are a hell of a lot fresher. Too bad we didn't get a better one."

"Maybe that Lola gave us a tired horse on purpose," Garrity said.

"No doubt," Wildon said angrily.

Garrity continued his candor. "This is a last stand, Lieutenant. We ain't getting out of this. If

180

we surrender, it'll only prolong the certainty of what's to happen."

"The sons of bitches will pay plenty though," Wildon said in dogged determination.

"There's something else to consider, sir," Garrity said. "I'm talking about your wife. It ain't pretty, sir, but you got to save the last bullet for her."

Wildon's eyes opened wide. "For the love of God! You mean *kill* her!"

"Yes, sir. You know what they'll do before they murder her if you don't take her out gentle and quick."

"Why?" Wildon asked. "Didn't that woman Lola say the bandit leader loved her? Hell, he didn't do anything bad to Hester while she was his prisoner. Why would he turn mean now?"

"The sonofabitch won't have no choice, sir," Garrity explained. "He's going to have to show his men that he isn't a softy. We've killed a lot of them too. He can't let none of us off. Not even Mrs. Boothe."

Wildon gritted his teeth. "God!"

"He'll give her to his men, sir," Garrity said. "You want her to endure that during her last hours of life?" He grabbed the lieutenant's shoulders. "God damn it! I've seen the results of these things."

Wildon nodded. "You're right, of course. Damn your eyes, Sergeant Garrity! You're always right, aren't you?"

"In this case it don't pleasure me much, sir," Garrity said solemnly.

A slight trembling in the ground could be discerned. The two soldiers looked over the rim of the arroyo. Out in the desert, coming on ten men abreast, the bandit gang pressed toward them.

"Maybe they'll ride by," Wildon said hopefully.

"No, sir," Garrity said. "You can tell from the direction they're coming that they've been to the village. Those poor folks there told on us."

"I guess I can't blame them," Wildon said. He looked back. "We've got about fifteen minutes left." He held out his hand. "Good-bye, Sergeant Garrity."

"So long, sir."

Wildon looked back at Hester. He wanted to go over to her, but there wasn't time. She had eased back into a cut in the arroyo wall. The opening was just large enough for her and the three horses. He waved at her and smiled.

The lieutenant looked back at the approaching enemy. They had drawn much closer. He cocked the Winchester, chambering a round. His hand reached down and touched the handle of his revolver, the awful words running through his mind.

The last bullet.

CHAPTER 17

The bandits charged toward the arroyo as a close-packed, thundering mob. The two soldiers knew exactly how to handle such an attack.

They fired evenly spaced shots, swinging the muzzles of their rifles to crisscross the broad target roaring down on them. The tactic spilled a dozen desperados from their mounts. The unfortunate outlaws hit the ground, rolling and bouncing before coming to undignified stops. They were covered with white dust that stuck to their blood-soaked clothing.

When the attackers swept past on each side of the arroyo, Wildon and Garrity changed positions to fire into their backs. Five more of Mauveaux's men were hit by the flying slugs.

The bandits rode fifty yards past the defended position, then turned off to the west, keeping plenty of range between themselves and the two soldiers.

Wildon slid his head above the arroyo and

watched their wide circuit. "They're keeping their distance," he said. "Looks like they've been stung enough to make them cautious."

"I'll say," Garrity said, remembering his own ambushes. "But they'll regroup for another assault."

Hester joined the two men. "I've hobbled the horses with the restraints you had in your saddlebags," she said. "They were getting hard to hold down."

"They're skittish and blowed," Garrity said. "All this noise ain't doing much for their dispositions."

Hester spoke as a horsewoman genuinely concerned about the faithful animals. "They are in need of a long rest. As of this moment, we cannot depend too much on the poor horses." She sighed. "They could never outrun Mauveaux's men."

"Mauveaux?" Wildon asked. "I thought the man's name was Mobo. Isn't that what the Mexican woman in the village told us?"

"Yes, sir," Garrity said. "But you gotta remember that the Spanish 'v' and 'b' are real close. It just sounded like Mobo to us."

"He is French," Hester said. "A former officer in their army. He told me he was going to be an emperor of an empire that stretched from here to South America."

"A mad man," Wildon said.

"But a gentleman, I must most hesitantly admit," Hester said. She thought it best not to bring up his amorous advances to her husband. "He treated me rather well, I must say."

"The Mexican lady said he was quite fond of you," Wildon said with a hint of jealousy in his voice.

Hester was a bit embarrassed at learning Wildon had been told about her former captor's affections. "Well—I suppose he was."

Garrity interrupted any further conversation. "Here they come again!"

"Get back with the horses, darling," Wildon said.

A distant thundering of hooves gradually grew louder. Both soldiers positioned themselves to meet the new attack. Wildon licked his dry lips. "They're spaced out more now."

"They're learning," Garrity said.

"So our bandit leader Mauveaux was an officer in the French army," Wildon mused.

Garrity laughed. "He must not have been a very damned good one. We've been tearing hell out of his command."

"Now isn't that a hell of a way to treat an emperor?" Wildon asked with sardonic humor.

The bandits swept on toward them. They were shouting and shooting, the inaccurate fire slapping through the air above the cavalrymen's heads.

Wildon picked out a particularly large individual. He laid the sights of the Winchester on the man's neck, taking care to allow for the bouncing of the riding target. When the time was right, he fired.

The bullet struck the outlaw's upper chest, abruptly knocking him straight back. The man's legs shot up as he went over his horse's rump.

Garrity's Henry now barked in evenly spaced shots. He swung the muzzle to the left with each squeeze of the trigger while Wildon went to the right.

Some of the bandits hit were in the ranks farther back because of their gapped formation. A total of five had gone down when the ragged formation suddenly turned and swept once again to the west. But this time they performed the maneuver in front of the soldiers. Rather than riding past and being unable to fire, they passed in front of the two Americans, eagerly shooting at their position.

"Goddamn their eyes!" Garrity shouted, ducking for cover.

Wildon did likewise as dozens of bullets splattered dirt over them in white clouds. The lieutenant spat, looking back where Hester was concealed. "Are you all right, dear?"

Hester waved to him from behind Garrity's horse.

The sergeant shoved some more shells into the Henry. "How's your ammunition doing, sir?"

"It's getting on the low side," Wildon said.

"We're gonna have to slow down," Garrity said.

"The only thing that's keeping the blackguards off us is the amount of bullets we throw out there at them," Wildon said. "If we cut back on our rate of fire, they're going to come in here like banshees from Hades."

"We ain't got a whole lot of choice at this point, Lieutenant," Garrity said. "Rapid fire is only going to hurry up what can't be avoided."

"You mean certain death," Wildon flatly stated.

"That's it exactly," Garrity said. "We can make this thing last as long as possible, or we can bring it to one hell of a finish."

"Let's not set any rules at this point," Wildon said. "Our instincts should take us along quite well."

Garrity pointed to Wildon's pistol. "The last bullet. Yours or mine?"

Wildon's mind had fought the reality of the situation to the point he had pushed the awful truth from his thoughts. His temper snapped. "God damn you, Sergeant Jim Garrity! I said let's let nature take its course. We'll do whatever is best at the most opportune time, won't we?"

"You still gotta keep what's to be done in the back of your mind," Garrity said. "And, Lieutenant Wildon Boothe, it's *got* to be done."

Further conversation was interrupted by a fresh attack.

187

Once more the bandits came straight on in a widespread formation. Riding hard, they leaned low over their horses' heads, their pistols aimed straight ahead.

"No long guns, Lieutenant!" Garrity shouted. "That means they want to close up. Get that pistol ready!"

Wildon fired two rounds from the Winchester, then ducked back down and pulled his pistol from its holster. Cocking the hammer, he crouched, waiting. He looked across to Garrity who had done the same thing.

The sound of the pounding hooves built up to a roaring crescendo. Finally the trembling of the earth caused by the galloping horses made bits of dirt fall from the arroyo's sides. When the din was so deafening it seemed to engulf them, the two soldiers stood up and cut loose with their pistols.

The targets at that close range were easy. On a couple of occasions it was horses that were hit, but most of the time it was bandit blood that splattered off into the desert air. Some collapsed lifeless, but a couple who had been wounded shouted curses and pulled away to ride out of the fight.

Then the bandit force split in two.

Each group swept around one side of the position, firing into the arroyo. Bullets spat and kicked up dirt, and ricochets zinged off into space.

"Holy Mother of God!" Garrity shouted, his Irish soul speaking out.

The hail of lead was short-lived but frightening, leaving the ground around them badly torn up. Both men, without saying it aloud, thought they were lucky to have come unscathed through the fusillade.

Wildon started to lean against the arroyo bank to get his breath. He sighted the bandit charging in on Garrity's side. "Get down," he yelled, picking up the Winchester. There was no time to aim and fire. The lieutenant simply grasped the weapon by the muzzle and stepped forward.

The bandit, firing wildly, galloped into their area. Wildon swung hard, the butt of the carbine sailing over the horse's head and hitting the outlaw straight on the chest. The man came out of the saddle and, rolling upside down, came down straight on his head.

The loud crack heralded his broken neck.

"Jump back, Lieutenant!"

Wildon didn't bother to look around, he simply obeyed.

Garrity, holding his pistol in both hands, fired three times.

Wildon's head snapped around to see the three *bandidos* coming down the arroyo from the opposite direction. One pitched from his horse. Another leaned forward and grasped his mount's neck to hang on. A blood spot was visible on his left side. The third man's luck was good. He swept by without harm, riding out on the far side of the ravine.

Once again it was quiet.

Garrity's face was covered with white dust. Sweat coming from beneath his hat streaked through it, leaving milky tracks down his cheeks. "We whipped 'em again."

"Yeah," Wildon said. He checked his ammunition. "We can hold them off maybe one more time."

"Yes, sir."

Wildon pulled the final rounds from his cartridge belt and reloaded his revolver. There was no need to say what he was going to use the weapon for. He picked up the Winchester. It held a half-dozen cartridges. "How's your Henry?"

"Like you said. One more time." He paused, letting Wildon say what had to be said.

The lieutenant took a deep breath. "I'd appreciate it, if you'd let me fire off the Winchester first, Sergeant Garrity. Then you can cover me with the Henry while I—" He paused and took a deep breath. "While I do what I must do."

"Yes, sir."

"Damn!"

"I'll see you have the time."

Wildon held out his hand. When Garrity took it, the young officer smiled. "By God we tried."

190

"By God we did."

Wildon went up into position while Garrity squatted down to wait his turn. The lieutenant looked out over the desert. There were no bandits in sight. He took a deep breath.

"Come on, you sons of bitches!"

The quiet continued after the echoes of his shouted challenge died away into the distance.

Finally the dull pounding of hooves sounded far away.

"Aim careful, sir," Garrity counseled.

"Yes, Sergeant." Wildon could see the smear of dust rising on the horizon.

"Remember to go for the upper chest while they're a ways out," the sergeant said. "The rounds'll drop into their bellies."

"Right," Wildon replied. "Maybe some of the wretches can roll around a bit before they die."

The dust cloud had grown considerably, and it was easy to see the riders causing it. Wildon raised the Winchester and picked out one of the men in the lead. He placed the sights just below his neck. After taking a couple of breaths, he stopped his breathing and gently worked the trigger.

The man's arms flew up, and he appeared to leap from the saddle.

Wildon grinned and worked the cocking lever. His eyes swept across the bandit gang. One fellow with a bright yellow bandanna around his neck caught the lieutenant's attention. Wildon spat and again swung up the muzzle of the carbine. A moment later he fired it.

The *bandido* turned violently sideways, then tried to straighten up. But he kept leaning farther and farther out until he finally slipped to the ground, performing a violent somersault when he contacted the desert floor.

Wildon chambered another cartridge.

Within a space of ten seconds, the third and fourth victims had been dealt with.

Garrity, still on his haunches, glanced up. "How's it going, Lieutenant?"

Wildon rubbed his chin. "Not too bad." A tall gangly man got the next bullet. "I can get one more," he announced to the sergeant.

"Be my guest, sir."

"Thank you." Wildon spotted a particularly aggressive fellow who was threading his way forward through the crowd of his fellow outlaws. The cavalry officer waited until the man had not only gotten through the mob, but was the leading rider. Waiting a couple of beats, he aimed the Winchester and fired.

The bandit's head appeared to explode, a geyser of red spurting out of one side of his skull.

Wildon stepped down. "They're all yours, Sergeant."

"Thank you, sir."

Wildon set the empty Winchester down. He

could see the cut in the ravine where Hester was hiding with the horses. Garrity was already firing as the lieutenant walked toward his wife, slowly pulling the Colt from the holster.

CHAPTER 18

Wildon, keeping himself from his wife's sight, walked close to the wall of the ravine next to her hiding place. When he reached the opening, he stopped, holding the revolver in his hand. The distraught young man took a deep breath to steady himself.

It was such a bizarre, unrealistic situation. How could anyone have known at their wedding a few short months before that the groom would soon slay the bride? Or how would it have been possible to have seen the two playing together as children to realize that in the distant future they would be facing death in a ravine in the wilds of Mexico, surrounded by a gang of cutthroats?

Waves of guilt swept through the young man. It was all his fault that such a wonderful girl was going to meet so cruel an end. He now felt his desires to be a soldier to be boyish and stupid.

Wildon shook his head to clear his thoughts. This was no time for a muddled mind. He had to think of the best way to do it. He would find it impossible to sneak into the small area without her seeing him. Yet he could not force himself to simply walk up and shoot her straight away with those big, beautiful green eyes staring at him. Finally, the best way to perform the awful deed occurred to him.

He would embrace his love, then ease the pistol up to the back of her skull and pull the trigger.

With any luck at all, the same bullet would kill him too.

Garrity fired again as Wildon stepped out and walked to the cut in the arroyo. When he stepped inside, he found Hester standing there. She had removed the hobbles from the horses, holding onto the reins in her small hands.

She smiled bravely at him. "I thought we might be going to try riding away again, so I got the horses ready."

"That was a good idea, dear," he lied. "We think we can make it this time." He walked up to Hester, slipping his arms around her, and gently pulled her to him. "I love you."

"I love you too, darling," Hester replied. She looked up into his face. "Don't worry, Wildon my love, we'll get out of this."

"Of course we will," he said. He gently placed his hand on the back of her head and pressed it to his chest. Taking a deep breath, he slowly raised the pistol and put the muzzle a few inches from the nape of her neck. He took care to make sure the bullet would fire upward and cause instant death. Once again he said, "I love you."

His finger tightened on the trigger.

A fresh roar of gunfire broke out above.

"Lieutenant!" Garrity called. "Lieutenant Boothe!"

Thankful for the interruption, Wildon stepped back, releasing his hold on Hester. He ran from the hiding place and joined the sergeant. "What's going on?" Suddenly he realized that the shooting out in the desert was not at them. "Who's out there, Sergeant Garrity?"

"Yaquis," Garrity said. "A bunch of the most beautiful goddamned ugly Yaqui Injuns you ever saw!" The excitement he showed was alien to his usual calm demeanor. "There must be fifty of the sonofabitches."

Wildon cautiously raised his head up to see what was going on. He saw a large number of mounted Indians riding among the bandits. Both groups fired indiscriminately at each other in a frenzy of wild, uncontrolled fighting. "Are they here to help us?" he asked.

Garrity shook his head. "No, sir. They don't even know we're over here. If they did, we'd be in the same fix as those goddamned *bandidos*."

"I wonder where they came from," Wildon remarked. "And what the hell are they doing attacking the bandits?"

"They're from the same group as that Injun that jumped you back on Bandido Mountain," Garrity said. "They musta finally found the fell-

196

er's body. No doubt they figger them bandits done him in. So they trailed 'em here."

"How could they track them?" Wildon asked. "Remember that's the area where we lost the trail."

"Hell, sir," Garrity told him, "a Yaqui or Apache Injun could track a lizard across solid rock." He looked over and saw Hester peering out of the cut. "Thank God you didn't do it."

"Do what?" Wildon asked. He knew that for the rest of his days he would try to deny not only to Garrity, but to himself that he had meant to kill his beloved Hester. He also knew he could never fool himself. This was an emotional torture to which he was condemned for all his days.

"Never mind, sir. Let's get the hell outta here."

The two rushed over to Hester and the mounts. Garrity took the bandit horse's reins.

"What is happening?" Hester asked.

"We don't have time to go into detail, darling," Wildon said. "But unexpected help arrived."

"Follow me," Garrity told them. He led his horse down the arroyo, turning north until he reached a point that led to solid ground. "Okay, folks," he said. "Let's mount up and ride."

Following his instructions, they got into the saddles. The hours of rest in the ravine had given their mounts a breather. Now, a bit fresher, the animals once again displayed an eagerness to run. Although they weren't in top form, they could

197

still gallop with respectable determination.

Wildon glanced back toward the impromptu battle going on to the south. The bandits and their Indian enemies were now closely intermingled. Hand-to-hand fighting had broken out in the vicious combat.

"They ain't gonna notice us," Garrity shouted. "But we got to clear the horizon. Ride!"

Wildon stuck close to Hester. The moment of truth again swept over him. Facts were facts, and the realization that he'd come so close to killing her churned painfully in his heart. If he had gone to perform the awful deed a minute earlier, he would have shot her only to find it had been all for nothing. The thought frightened him more than anything else had done during the entire rescue and escape.

But denial once again rushed through his mind. He wouldn't have done it, he told himself, not in a thousand years. Almost weeping, he forced himself to concentrate on the flight to freedom.

Fifteen minutes later, they could tell there would be no pursuit. Even if the Yaquis discovered where they had been, the three would have a comfortable enough lead to be across the border and back in the United States before the fierce Indians could hope to catch up with them.

An hour later, cantering at a regular pace northward, Garrity made the happy announcement. "We're outta Mexico."

"Thank the good Lord that is over," Hester said.

The sun was a red disk as it eased down on the western side of the Santo Domingos. The color seemed apropos after such a bloody day on the desert.

Hubert Mauveaux drank his coffee and stared into the flames of the campfire. The bandit leader glanced up when his name was called out.

Paco Fuentes joined his chief, squatting down and helping himself to the coffee. *"Bueno, mi general,* the situation is not the best."

Mauveaux, sullen, looked out over the bivouac where the survivors of the day's fighting were finishing up their evening meal. "What is the matter with the dogs? Have they been so badly whipped that their tails are between their legs?"

"The men are very confused," Paco explained. "I have been talking to many of them. None expected the two *gringos* to fight like such devils, nor did they expect the Yaquis to join in the battle."

Mauveaux reached inside his shirt and withdrew a cigar. He bit off the end and spat. "I will give ten thousand pesos to anyone who can explain to me why those Indians suddenly appeared and attacked us."

"No one but the Yaquis could tell us that,"

Paco said. "And they are all dead."

"At a terrible cost to my army," Mauveaux said.

"Most of your soldiers now wish to return to *Montaña Bandido*," Paco said. "Many have died today, some are hurt, yet nobody has earned one centavo for all of that."

"Mercenaires!" Mauveaux exclaimed. "Are they not satisfied to follow my orders? Do they not know that I shall lead them to greatness?"

"Perdoname, mi general," Paco said, "but many of the men are not as devoted as myself."

"You are a loyal subject, Paco," Mauveaux said. "And you shall be well rewarded."

"Gracias, mi general."

Paco had been one of the first to join up when the Frenchman formed his gang. He'd liked Mauveaux's style from the start. Although not much of a battle commander, the ex-officer was a good planner. He could coordinate train robberies, pick out particularly vulnerable haciendos for plundering, and intercept gold shipments with uncanny skill. Paco knew that if anything bad ever happened to Mauveaux, his own fortunes would decline because of it.

Mauveaux finished his coffee. "You look like a man with something on his mind, Paco."

"I have, *mi general,*" Paco Fuentes said. "I would like to point out something to you in a most respectful manner."

200

"Ah! You offer me counsel and advice? Please, I have valued your wise recommendations for several years now."

"Thank you," Fuentes said. "What I wish to discuss with you is an unpleasant fact. It would seem to me that you must react to this latest situation in a rapid and ruthless manner, *mi general.*"

"Explain yourself."

"The situation with the American woman has made you look most vulnerable," Fuentes said diplomatically. "I fear many of the men think you made a fool of yourself over the woman."

"Of course," Mauveaux agreed. "Those dolts are not soulful beings with sentiment and tenderness in their hearts. They are boors and savages no better than animals."

"Yes, *mi general,* but you need them to make your empire," Fuentes said. He knew the empire-building scheme was insanity, but as long as successful robberies kept Mauveaux in gold and women, Paco was more than ready to encourage his leader to keep going. "So you must keep the soldiers satisfied."

Mauveaux was thoughtful for several moments. "Of course. Even the emperors of Rome had to placate the Praetorian guard."

"There are two things that must be done," Fuentes continued. "The first thing is to continue the pursuit after the American woman."

201

"But she will only go back to the useless baggage train," Mauveaux said. "There is no loo there."

"*Es verdad* — that is true," Fuentes said. "Whe you announce your intention to attack ther again, only your best men will follow you. Th others will return to Bandido Mountain."

"What is the point then?"

"The point, *mi general*, is that when you retur to our town with the woman, it will bring you prestige back to where it was," Fuentes argued "The reluctant swine among your soldiers wil once again be loyal and steadfast."

"And if I don't bring her back, some upstar will challenge my authority," Mauveaux said, a the truth of the situation dawned on him.

"You have been thought of as soft because o your affections for the *americana*," Fuentes con tinued. "You must show you are a merciless war rior king."

"Emperor," Mauveaux corrected him. "I am a merciless warrior emperor."

"*Seguro que si,*" Fuentes agreed. "To show yo are without compassion for those who wrong you give the woman to the men."

Mauveaux's affections for Hester Boothe had already faded rapidly since her escape. He shrugged. *"Comment non?* I was going to do tha anyway, of course. She will be no more than a common camp prostitute."

202

"That is the way to be," Fuentes said. "Do you wish to speak to the men now?"

"Call them together," Mauveaux said.

Paco Fuentes first went to the most loyal bandits. Getting a half-dozen to follow him around, he visited each small campfire telling the outlaws there that their leader wished to speak to them. Most accepted the announcement quietly, only slightly annoyed at the interruption of their evening meal. Others were more hostile, but said nothing because of the escort Fuentes had brought with him.

One man, a big American named Scanlon, found the situation very interesting. When Fuentes came to his campsite, he spat into the flames. "What's on the chief's mind, Paco?"

"He'll tell you, Scanlon," Fuentes replied coldly. "You be there."

Scanlon, over six feet tall, reached down and grasped Fuentes' vest. "Ain't you even gonna give me a hint, Paco? I'd hate to leave my supper and go all the way over there to hear something I ain't inter'sted in."

Fuentes pulled himself free. "You're starting to talk *muy grande,* Scanlon. I would watch it, if I were you."

"Well," Scanlon said. "You ain't me, are you, Paco?"

Fuentes knew a showdown was looming. He finished making his rounds, then returned to

Mauveaux. He found his chief drinking more cof
fee and smoking a fresh cigar. Fuentes bent down
and whispered in the Frenchman's ear, pointing
over to where Scanlon stood by the fire
Mauveaux listened intently, nodding in complete
understanding.

Fifteen minutes later the survivors of the bandit
gang were gathered around their leader's campfire
Most squatted or sat down in the dirt, making
themselves comfortable. The one noticeable excep-
tion was Scanlon. He stood tall and menacing,
his arms folded across his massive chest, the expression on his face displaying contempt and arrogance.

Mauveaux calmly finished his coffee, then
tossed the remnants of the cigar into the fire. He
turned and walked toward his men. The bandit
leader's hand dropped to his pistol, and he drew
it in a smooth, lightning-quick motion. He fired
it twice, both bullets striking Scanlon.

The big American bent double, holding onto
his slug-mutilated chest, then collapsed to the
ground. One booted foot twitched several times,
then was still.

Mauveaux calmly returned the pistol to his holster. "Now that I have your attention," he said. "I
will tell you of my plans for the next few days."

All eyes were respectfully turned on *el general*.

CHAPTER 19

Quartermaster Sergeant Tom Mulvaney could barely hear the flanker's shout over the sound of the stiff breeze playing across the Llano Estacado. He turned with his hand cupped over his ear in order to hear better. The soldier repeated the call.

"Riders coming in, Sergeant!"

Mulvaney turned his horse from its position at the head of the wagon train and galloped over to the flanker. "Goddamn it! Where're they at, Rampey? I don't see nothing."

"They went down in a draw to the south," the young trooper reported. "They ought to show up any time now." He kept looking in the direction where he pointed. For a few moments the desert scenery remained bare. "Look! There they are!"

Mulvaney pulled his field glasses from their case and focused them in. "By all the saints!" he exclaimed. He looked again, studying the scene to make sure his eyes were not tricked by the dancing heat waves. "Yes, by God! It's them! It's Mis-

ter Boothe and his wife. And there's Jim Garrit
riding just behind 'em."

Rampey took off his hat and let out a chee
"Hoorah! Hoorah! They brung her back!"

Others in the wagon train now shouted to on
another as the happy news was passed from vehi
cle to vehicle.

"They're back!"

"It's the lieutenant and Sergeant Garrity!"

"Mrs. Boothe is with 'em! They got her!"

Mulvaney ordered the wagons to halt. Next he
shouted to the two men on rear guard. "Dort
mann! Jones! Ride out and escort 'em in."

The two veterans waved their compliance. They
turned toward the three people in the distance
and kicked their mounts' flanks. As they drew
closer, they could see one of them waving his ha
back and forth in greeting.

"That's Sergeant Garrity," Dortmann called ou
to Jones. "He'll be in a bad temper after all that,
I'll wager."

"I can see the lieutenant and his missus," Jones
yelled back. "God! I'm surprised they was able to
get her."

"I always figgered Lieutenant Boothe had
sand," Dortmann hollered. "But I never knowed
he was this good."

"He had Garrity with him," Jones reminded his
pal.

"Maybe so, but I'll bet the sarge didn't do it

all alone while the lieutenant sat around and watched," Dortmann countered.

It took them five minutes to reach the arrivals. Both troopers saluted properly and reported in to Wildon.

"Good afternoon, Troopers," Wildon said. "We appreciate the escort."

"Our pleasure, sir," Dortmann replied.

"How're you, Sergeant Garrity?" Jones asked. All three of the recent arrivals looked exhausted and dirty.

"Straighten up that saddleroll," Garrity said. "You'll lose the thing in another five miles of riding."

"Yes, Sergeant," Jones replied, turning slightly to tend to the chore. "I see things ain't changed," he said to Dortmann.

"What was that?" Garrity asked.

"I said I'm changing the roll," Jones said lamely.

"Fix it later," Garrity said. "We're in a bad way for drinking water."

Back in the wagon train Mulvaney had gone to his wagon and informed his wife Dixie of what had transpired. Dixie knew exactly what she wanted to do. "Bring Mrs. Boothe over to me, Tom," she instructed.

"You sure you want me to?" he asked. "She didn't show a lot o' friendlies toward you if I recall."

"Don't you mind none o' that a'tall," Dixie said. She expertly stepped from the seat onto the wheel and let herself down to the ground. "Sadie! Mary! Nancy! Come here quickly!"

The other enlisted wives in the train—Sadie Tannon, Mary Dougherty, and Nancy Mason— climbed down from their own vehicles and quickly walked over to join Dixie.

"Lieutenant Boothe and Jim Garrity are back with Mrs. Boothe," Dixie quickly explained.

"Lord above!" Sadie said. "The poor, dear woman. Have you seen her yet, Dixie?"

"No, but I told Tom to bring her here," Dixie said. "She don't need the rough comp'ny o' men now."

"That's for sure," Sadie Tannon agreed. "Remember that rancher woman after the patrol brung her in from the Apaches? She'd suffered something awful."

"But what about the surgeon?" Mary asked.

"That drunk!" Dixie said. "The likes o' him ain't gonna do Mrs. Boothe a bit o' good."

"But she may have suffered so," Mary enjoined. "She could be bad hurt."

"Then it's a hurt we'll fix," Dixie said. "But it'll be more the injury of her woman's soul and dignity. Only her and the Lord knows what's been through."

"She isn't the nicest officer's lady I've ever known," Nancy Mason said, "but my heart goes out to her."

"I have some tea," Mary Dougherty offered.

"Fetch it, dear," Dixie said.

A loud cheer came from the wagons as Wildon, Hester, and Garrity rode in with their escorts. Dixie and Sadie scampered forward, pushing their way through the crowd of soldiers and teamsters who had gathered around the arrivals. Dixie wasted no time grabbing hold of Hester. "Come this way, dear, if you please."

Hester's face lit up with a broad smile. Dixie and Sadie were welcome sights, their Irish faces a pleasing contrast to what she'd been exposed to for the previous weeks. "Why, hello, Mrs. Mulvaney, Mrs. Thompson."

"We've some nice tea brewing," Dixie said.

The two enlisted wives flanked Hester as they led her back to the Mulvaney wagon. "How are you feeling, Mrs. Boothe?" Sadie asked.

"I am exhausted!" Hester proclaimed. "You can't imagine what it's been like."

"Poor, poor darling," Dixie cooed at her.

The women joined Mary and Nancy at the Mulvaney wagon, who rushed forward. Hester, a bit confused but appreciating the solicitous treatment, greeted them with a bright smile. "So nice to see you again."

"Tea is brewing now," Mary said. "We'll give you a cup in just a moment."

"Thank you," Hester said. "A nice cup of tea

will be delightful."

"I only wish we had water to let you wash," Nancy said.

"I had a chance to take a bath a few nights ago," Hester said. "There was soap, towels, and hot water."

Dixie, now afraid the younger woman might be delirious, helped her to sit down on a camp stool. "Are you comfortable there, Mrs. Boothe?"

"Yes. Thank you so much."

"It would be perfectly all right if you wanted to lie down in my wagon," Dixie said.

"This is fine," Hester said. "And the thought of that tea is making my head spin."

"It won't be long now," Mary sang out.

Dixie decided it was time to get down to cases. "Now, Mrs. Boothe. We're your friends, you understand that?"

"Oh, yes! I do appreciate this kind reception you've given me, really," Hester said.

"Yes, dear," Dixie said wanting to be delicate. "How are you feeling?"

"Well, like I said, very tired," Hester replied.

"What I mean, dear Mrs. Boothe, is—are you in pain?"

"Oh, no."

"No bleeding?" Dixie asked. "Or cuts and bruises that want tending to? Now be sure, and don't you fret. We'll take care o' things. There's no reason a'tall to call the surgeon."

"No," Hester replied, not quite understanding the type of injuries Dixie Mulvaney was referring to.

Sadie put an arm around the young woman. "We're your friends, Mrs. Boothe. You may tell us."

"Tell you what?" Hester asked.

"What you need done," Sadie said. "Don't worry. We won't let the surgeon touch you."

Nancy Mason decided to be more direct. "What happened to you while those awful bandits had you, Mrs. Boothe?"

Sadie was shocked. "Nancy!"

Hester smiled. "Well I was proposed to."

"Proposed to!" the four women exclaimed in unison.

Hester giggled. "Yes! Their leader wanted me to marry him. He even proposed to make me his empress."

Dixie leaned forward. "Didn't he outrage you, Mrs. Boothe? Didn't any of his men force themselves on you?"

"Dear me, no!" Hester exclaimed. "In fact, Mister Mauveaux was a perfect gentleman." She paused. "Well, not perfect. He was most familiar with many of his remarks. And he was certainly rude when he referred to my Wildon."

. Mary Dougherty handed Hester a cup of tea. "I, for one, would like to hear about this romantic bandit chief."

211

"He and his men live on a mountain top," Hester began. "Mister Mauveaux is a Frenchman and his house—he calls it a castle—is the biggest in the town they have there."

"Saints above!" Mary Dougherty exclaimed. "I remember such a place when I was but a small girl in Ireland. Made of stone it was, with towers and turrets and an immense inner court."

Sadie Tannon laughed. "If he'd proposed to me, I might have given it some serious thought."

"It sounds romantic," Dixie added.

"Not really," Hester said. "But he did have a violinist come in for dinner."

"It sounds like you had a lovely time," Mary Dougherty said.

"Oh, not at all," Hester said. "There was something evil about him and that awful place. Many of the people there had diabolical auras about them. It's difficult to describe."

Surgeon Schuyler Dempster, a bit tipsy, walked up to the ladies. "G'd afternoon, I am seeking Mrs. Boothe."

Dixie did not hide her disapproval. "And what would a lady want with a drunken doctor?"

Dempster ignored the open insult. "I only came to see if she required medical attention."

"Sure and none that you would have to offer," Mary Dougherty said. "Off with you now. This is woman's talk here."

"I prefer to speak to the lady in question,"

Dempster said.

Hester smiled at him. "I am just fine, Doctor. My friends have fixed some nice tea for me."

"Very well," Dempster said. "At any rate, it is not difficult to see I am not welcome in this place."

Hester watched him walk away. "Oh, ladies. That was most unkind."

"He's a good and caring doctor when he's sober and that's a fact," Dixie said. "But when the man is in his cups, he's a butcher."

"That's true," Sadie interjected. "We've told him before that he won't be tolerated when he's drunk. We've been brutally honest with him."

"I see," Hester said. "There is so much I have to learn about the regiment and its people." She hesitated, then spoke out. "I am afraid I've not done my best to fit in. I'm truly sorry about that."

Dixie smiled. "Now don't you worry none, dear Mrs. Boothe."

"Sure and you're one o' the regimental officers' ladies now," Mary Dougherty said.

"Thank you," Hester said. "Thank you for the kindness and the care you've shown me. I shan't forget it ever."

Sergeant Mulvaney indicated a point on the map. "Here's our location now, sir. As you can

213

see, we've still a good twelve to fourteen days o' travel left before we get to Fort Mojave."

Wildon, back in uniform now, inspected the map. "The journey is going to get rougher once we're out of the Llano Estacado. Looks like mountains there."

"Indeed, sir," Garrity said. "No high peaks, but plenty of steep climbing just the same."

The three were gathered in the shade of the supply wagon. Wildon learned that a total of three men had been killed in the initial bandit raid. Two were teamsters. The problem created by the loss of the wagon drivers was solved by detailing one trooper from the escort to act as a driver. The second wagon was hooked to another and its team of mules harnessed in to help pull the extra load.

"Do you think them outlaws will come back at us?" Mulvaney asked.

"I doubt it," Wildon said.

"The lowlife bastards didn't find nothing worth stealing the first time," Garrity reasoned. "Why come back for another load of nothing?"

"Maybe those Yaquis wiped them out," Wildon suggested.

"Could be," Garrity said. "Or maybe they all massacred each other."

"At any rate, we're still due at Fort Mojave," Wildon said. "So let's move out."

"Yes, sir!"

Both N.C.O.s saluted and went to their posts. Wildon walked over to his wagon where his horse was tied. Hester had left her friends and now sat on the seat with the teamster. She waved to her husband. "Are we ready to renew our journey?"

"We certainly are," Wildon said. "We'll all be much better off once we're at the new garrison." He mounted his horse and rode up to the front of the wagon train. Turning back to face the vehicles and people, he gave the order to proceed. "Forward, *yo-oh!*"

Wildon settled into the ride. But he had trouble concentrating on the task ahead. His mind raced with confusion and new attitudes and considerations of his wife and the army.

Perhaps he should resign his commission and return to New York with Hester. My God! his thoughts told him. He'd come within a few seconds of actually killing her to keep the poor young woman from being raped and brutalized by a gang of border bandits. What sort of life had he brought her to? What right did he have to insist that she stay and live in such an awful place?

Perhaps the desire to be a soldier was no more than boyish, silly daydreams that should now be dashed by reality. Their life at Fort Mojave would be no better than what they endured at Fort MacNeil. And what about the next miserable post? And the next? And the next? The awful circumstances of frontier service could go on for the next thirty years.

Wildon took a deep breath and made up his mind.

When they arrived at Fort Mojave, he would submit a resignation of his commission and return to New York to get into his family's business.

He glanced over to the flankers and saw Sgt. James Garrity riding there. Garrity grinned and waved back. A look to the other side showed the old troopers Dortmann and Jones guarding that flank.

Soldiers all.

A wave of disappointment and frustration swept through 2d Lt. Wildon Boothe. No matter how he rationalized or contemplated the situation, he loved the army and, above all, the United States Cavalry.

CHAPTER 20

Trooper Harold Rampey and his best pal Trooper David Mauson were stationed as flankers on the left side of the wagon train. Their former disappointment with army life due to constant demands of manual labor and boring stints of guard duty had been alleviated somewhat by the earlier fight with the bandits.

Although three men had been killed in the battle, the pair of eighteen-year-olds had already forgotten the horror of seeing comrades shot down. Their young minds spent more time dwelling on the thrill of exchanging shots with the desperados.

Harold pointed to the front where 2d Lt. Wildon Boothe rode. "There's a hell of an officer, David."

"He sure is," David replied in sincere tones. "Wasn't that something of him riding off and rescuing his wife from them outlaws? That's just like knights do in storybooks. Only they don't fetch their wives, they save damsels."

"Sergeant Garrity helped out," Harold reminded him."

"Yeah, but it was the lieutenant who was in charge," his friend said.

"She's a pretty lady," Harold said.

"Who?"

"Missus Boothe, you idjit! Don't you think she's grand?" he added, not realizing she was only a few months older than they.

"I bet you got a big crush on her, don't you?"

"No, I don't," Harold said.

"Yes, you do!"

"Don't!"

"Do!"

"Well, anyhow, she's pretty like I said," Harold insisted.

"Kinda snobbish though," David noted. "You ever see how she looks at us fellers? It's like we ain't even there sometimes."

"Oof!" Harold slumped in the saddle.

"What's the matter with you?"

The second shot was louder and whipped between them with a ripping sound. David looked in the distance. "Riders coming in!" he shouted. "C'mon, Harold!"

"I think I been shot, David," he said in a weak voice.

David looked at him. "You been hit in the back of the shoulder. Can you hang on?"

"I guess I better."

The two veterans, Dortmann and Jones, had been riding the rear guard. They heard the shot

218

and had seen Rampey sway in the saddle. The old soldiers knew exactly what had happened. Without uttering a word, they galloped out toward the two young troopers. With carbines drawn, Dortmann and Jones covered the kids' withdrawal back to the wagon train.

Lieutenant Boothe had also heard the shots. He came in quickly from his post at the head of the wagon train to join them. "Did either of you see where the shot came from?"

Dortmann, still on alert, shook his head. "No, sir, not exactly."

"It had to be from the southeast," Jones added.

Wildon noticed Harold and David sitting awkwardly on their horses. "Damn it, Mauson! Get Rampey down to the surgeon. He's bleeding."

"Yes, sir," David said. "C'mon, Harold."

The lieutenant got his field glasses and stood in the stirrups as he looked through the lenses at the far horizon.

"God damn them!" he exclaimed.

Dortmann squinted his eyes, trying to see in the distance. "What's out there, sir?"

"Those bandits have found us again," Wildon said. "Let's head back for the wagon train."

The trio of cavalrymen turned their horses and raced back to the vehicles. "Form a circle!" Wildon shouted. "Sergeant Garrity, bring in the other flankers."

Within short moments the small detachment was prepared to defend itself. The women were gathered around the Mulvaney wagon. This time rather than staying at their own vehicles, they stuck together in a group. This was Wildon's idea. He wanted none snatched up by the bandits. In keeping them together, they would be easier to watch over.

The soldiers and teamsters stood tensely at their posts. There was no movement out in the desert, only the sound of the wind whipping through the canvas tops of the wagons.

"Out there!" a soldier shouted. "Look!"

A half-dozen bandits appeared on the horizon. They rode in a wide circle around the train, but fired no shots and made no attempts to close in within rifle range. After making an obvious observation of the situation, they rode out of sight.

Sergeant Garrity, standing beside Wildon, spat a stream of tobacco juice. "They just wanted to see how we was setting up."

"Fine," Wildon said grimly. "Now the sons of bitches can come on in here and get killed."

"Damn right, sir."

But the next appearance of the outlaws was even more peaceful than the first. Two of them came into view — and they had a white flag.

"What the hell?" Wildon asked.

"I'd say they wanted a parley," Garrity said.

The two-man *bandido* delegation rode to a

point within a hundred yards of the soldiers. They waved the white flag. One of them then galloped toward the wagons holding his hands over his head. When he was within shouting distance, he stopped.

"I wish to speak with *el comandante!*" he hollered. He motioned to the man behind him to ride up. "I claim the protection of *la bandera blanca*—the white flag."

Wildon looked at Garrity. "What do you think, Sergeant? I never heard of hooligans calling a truce."

"I haven't either," Garrity said. "We'd best stay on the alert. It could be a trap. In the meantime, let's see what he's got to say," Garrity suggested.

Wildon waved to Sergeant Mulvaney. "Take over until we get back, Sergeant!"

"Yes, sir," Mulvaney said. "Watch for tricks, you two."

Wildon and Garrity mounted up. They rode out to the two bandits and stopped ten yards from them. The lieutenant was blunt. "Say your piece."

But the bandit insisted on protocol. "I am *Coronel* Paco Fuentes, the chief of staff for *el General* Mauveaux the *generalisimo* of the Latin Army."

Wildon crossed his arms and exhibited a sneer. "What do you want, Paco?" he asked, purposely using the man's first name.

"*Sí, tu*," Garrity said. "*Que quieres?*" He used the familiar pronoun rather than the respectful "*usted.*"

Fuentes frowned. "I am an officer like your selves," he insisted. "I have been made a *coronel.*

"Speak up, Paco," Wildon said. "We don't have all day."

"*Muy bien,*" Fuentes said angrily. "On behalf of *el General* Mauveaux I demand your immediate surrender."

"Most interesting," Wildon said. He yawned.

"Our army numbers in the hundreds," Fuentes continued. "We can crush you at any time. But the benevolent and merciful *el General* Mauveaux will grant you your lives. All you must do is surrender your arms and wagons. Then you will be allowed to continue unmolested on your way."

"Your boss's demand is asinine," Wildon said. "I reject it outright and will not even take such a ridiculous proposal under consideration."

Fuentes couldn't quite understand what the American lieutenant meant. "What is it you say to me?"

Garrity interrupted. "What he's saying is for you to piss up a rope."

"You refuse the demand of *el general?*" Fuentes asked.

Wildon drew his pistol and shoved the muzzle toward the Mexican's face. "You're got one minute to get out of here and crawl back under a rock, or I am going to blow your head off your shoulders, you son of a bitch."

Fuentes and his flag bearer wisely left the scene without further comment.

While Wildon and Garrity rode back toward the wagon train, Surgeon Dempster sought out Dixie Mulvaney. When he found her with the other ladies, he tipped his hat. "How do you do, Mrs. Mulvaney?" He held up a restraining hand before she spoke. "Now I'm sober as a judge right now." He sighed. "Unfortunately my hospital steward is not."

"You've not set a good example for him," Dixie said.

"Perhaps not, ma'am," Dempster admitted. "At any rate, I'll need some help from a couple of your ladies. Young Trooper Rampey has been hit in the shoulder, and I've got to get the bullet out and bandage him up. It's a bit more than I can accomplish on my own."

"Well, certainly, man. Why didn't you say so in the first place?" Dixie said.

Hester, standing nearby, spoke up. "I would be glad to lend a hand."

"Thank you kindly, Mrs. Boothe," Dempster said.

"I believe it's customary from what I've heard," Hester said. "I am the senior officer's wife."

Mary Dougherty stepped forward. "It's not necessary, Mrs. Boothe. I'd be happy to stand in for you."

"Thank you very much," Hester replied. "W army wives seem to have our duties as do ou husbands."

"I am grateful to you, Mrs. Boothe. Your hel is truly needed." Dempster replaced his hat an led the two women back to his ambulance. H had placed Rampey on an operating table tha consisted of a stretcher laid across some hardtac boxes. The young soldier was in pain, but h managed a weak smile for the ladies.

"How do, Missus Boothe, Missus Mulvaney," h said weakly.

"Now, young man, we're going to make you a better," Dempster said. He got his instrument cas and set it on the tailgate of the ambulance. "Let' see about giving you a nice nap."

Rampey gave the doctor a suspicious look "What are you going to do?"

"I'm just about to administer a nice soothin application of chloroform," Dempster said "You'll go to sleep and before you know it, you' be wide awake and it'll all be over."

He took a cloth and placed it across a smal wire frame just large enough to fit over a man' mouth and nose. After splashing on a few drop of chloroform, he set it down on the young pa tient's face. At first Rampey shook his head i protest, but quickly grew feeble and went t sleep.

"Now we must be fast," Dempster said. "Mrs. Mulvaney, will you be kind enough to sponge away the blood while I probe for the bullet?"

"Certainly," Dixie said. She knew exactly what to do. She went straight to the instrument kit and retrieved a sponge. "I'm ready."

"What do you require of me?" Hester asked a bit fearfully.

"Simply hold on to his wrist, Mrs. Boothe," Dempster said.

She did as she was told. "Yes?"

"Can you feel his pulse?"

Hester gingerly felt around. "Oh, yes. Now I can."

"Fine. Now if it begins to get very weak or erratic, please let me know," Dempster said. "Anesthetics sometimes act as more of a depressant than we desire." He took another look at the ladies. "Shall we begin?"

He gently rolled Rampey over to expose his wound. Using a foreign-body probe with a blunt end, the surgeon deftly inserted it into the bullet hole and gently eased it forward.

"If it weren't for the chloroform," he said cheerfully, "this young soldier would be screaming his head off about now."

Hester smiled weakly as she monitored the pulse. Dixie sponged at the blood pouring from the wound. "At least we've no problems with arteries this time," she said matter-of-factly.

Dempster glanced up at Hester. "Mrs. Mulvaney has aided me on countless such operations." He continued pressing the probe. "Ah! Here it is Not deep at all. The bullet must have been fired from a long range."

Hester was suddenly alarmed. "Doctor Dempster, the pulse is going away!"

Dempster grabbed the wrist and checked the rate. "It certainly is." He went to his kit and brought back a bottle of liquor of ammonia. Opening the stopper, he shoved it under Rampey's nose for a brief moment. "Any change now, Mrs Boothe?"

Hester nodded. "It's back to where it was."

"Fine. It's only a matter of a bit of stimulant to counter the chloroform," Dempster said. "Now. let's get that bullet out, hey?" Taking a pair of bullet forceps he went into the wound with a smooth swift motion since he knew exactly were to go. After working the instrument a bit, he withdrew it. "Look at that." He showed the ladies the bullet which was almost intact from not hitting bone. "I'd say that was a .50 caliber. Probably shot at our young hero here from a buffalo rifle of some sort."

"He's lucky," Dixie said.

Dempster put a compress over the wound. "Now hold him up so I can wind a nice tight bandage around the shoulder." The surgeon worked quickly, finally securing the cotton strips.

"A week or two in a sling, and Trooper Rampey will be back peeling potatoes and digging latrines."

They gently rolled the still unconscious soldier on his back. Dempster removed the anesthetic mask, and took his hat to begin an energetic fanning of Rampey's face. "We must purge that chloroform from his lungs," he said.

Within a few moments Rampey's eyelids fluttered. Finally he came wide awake and rolled over to vomit onto the ground. Hester had to jump back to avoid being splattered. Rampey stared around dull-eyed and drowsy. "When're you gonna start?" he asked in a slurred voice.

"Why, my boy, you are already on your way to a full recovery," Dempster said. "And guess what?"

"What?"

"I'm going to write out a light duty slip for you," Dempster said.

Rampey smiled lazily. "That's the bes' news I've had since I joined the army."

"Thank the ladies for helping out," the surgeon said.

More awake now, Rampey sat up. "Ow!"

"I've just been sticking probes in you, lad. Between that and the bullet, you'll be tender there for a while," Dempster said.

Now Rampey noticed the bandages. "Oh, yeah. I guess I'm fixed up." He looked at Dixie. "I

thank you most kindly, ma'am." The young
trooper turned his gaze to Hester. "You're a beautiful lady."

"He's still under the influence of the chloroform," Dempster said. "It removes inhibitions, but
in his case has not impaired his judgment."

Hester smiled at the compliment. "Come, Dixie.
Let us go back to the other ladies."

"I'm sure they'll have some nice hot coffee
waiting for us, Mrs. Boothe," Dixie said.

They walked across the small area. "Dixie,"
Hester said, "would you mind calling me by my
first name?"

Dixie smiled. "Not at all, Hester."

"Good." Hester said. "It will make our friend-
ship that much easier to grow, won't it?"

The afternoon dragged by in silence. There was
not a sign of the bandits out on the desert. No
scouting parties, no probing attacks, not even a
casual view of a careless outlaw.

Wildon had called a conference of war with the
two senior N.C.O.s. "They've got us locked in
here for the time being. I need to know our exact
situation. How's the water, Sergeant Mulvaney?"

"We'll be running into a problem soon, sir. If
we were rolling along on schedule, we'd be out of
the Llano Estacado in three more days. We
planned on finding fresh water then. As it is, we

228

can stay here maybe four days—five at the most."

"We'll begin rationing immediately. What about the food?"

"Two weeks' supply," Mulvaney said. "No problem."

"Fine," Wildon said. "I presume our ammunition supply is adequate."

"That's about all—adequate," Mulvaney said. "We can hold out and give 'em hell, but we ain't gonna do it for more'n a coupla days."

Wildon turned to Garrity. "How are the men, Sergeant?"

"We've got nine troopers and three teamsters, sir," Garrity said. "There's one man wounded. We also got the hospital orderly who's as useless and welcome as a whore at church call."

"The worthless bastard," Mulvaney spat. "He was too drunk to help out with young Rampey's operation earlier."

"Break him to the rank of trooper and hand him a carbine," Wildon said. "The ladies can help the surgeon if need be."

"Yes, sir," Garrity said.

Wildon glanced out beyond the circle of wagons. "Frankly, I didn't expect to see those bandits again."

"Neither did I, sir," Garrity admitted.

"I wonder how many of them there are," Wildon mused. "Do you suppose we could make a run for it?"

Garrity shook his head. "No, sir. From the way they're acting, that's what they want us to do."

"Then, Sergeant, we are under siege, are we not?"

"That we are, sir," Garrity said.

Mulvaney, ever the logistics man, looked around at their small force. "It's gonna be the old question of who can outlast who," the sergeant commented dryly.

CHAPTER 21

Thirty slow hours crept by while 2d Lt. Wildon Boothe's small command of troopers and wagons waited to see what the border renegades were going to do.

The hospital steward, a former medical student named Steiner, provided the only break in the monotony when Sgt. James Garrity dragged him unconscious from under the ambulance. Garrity didn't stop there. He had the drunk lashed to a wagon wheel to sober up under the hot rays of the Llano Estacado sun. It took four hours to bring the alcoholic around enough for Lieutenant Boothe to inform him he'd been reduced in rank. A failure at everything, Steiner took the news calmly, accepting the carbine someone shoved into his hands. After removing his gear from the ambulance, he went to his assigned place on the firing line to nurse his hangover.

Wildon Boothe and Sergeant Mulvaney made a physical check of the water barrels. Their level was down enough to cause them concern. The hot weather was going to make the shortage of water a serious problem. It was so grave, in fact that the lieutenant had to get something going Sitting on the desert was certainly not going to improve their circumstances. Once again, he called on the counsel and soldiering skills of Sgt James Garrity.

"There are two possibilities we must face up to," Wildon said. "One, the bandits are going to try to wait us out, then hit us after we've been badly weakened by lack of water. Or two, the fight they had with the Yaqui Indians have weakened them so much that they have withdrawn and are no longer a threat to us."

"We've got only one way to find out, sir," Garrity said. "I'll take a patrol and look for 'em. If the bastards are out there, we'll know they intend to give us a fight. If they've gone, we'll roll merrily along to Fort Mojave."

"Yes," Wildon agreed. "If they're still here we'll have to come up with a damned good and original plan on how to run and fight at the same time with a numerically superior enemy."

"I'll take Steiner and Mauson with me," Garrity said.

"I think you better take a couple of better men," Wildon suggested. "Steiner is a drunkard and Mauson is only a bit more than a recruit You might need a couple of old hands out there."

"Steiner and Mauson won't be much of a loss then, sir," Garrity said.

"Do you think it could be that bad?" Wildon asked.

"Yes, sir."

"We can't spare you, Sergeant Garrity," Wildon said. "Take care."

"You know I always do, Lieutenant," Garrity said with a grin. "I'll go get my patrol together."

"Good luck."

When Garrity detailed the two soldiers to the job, their attitudes toward the patrol were entirely different. Trooper Mauson took it as a compliment to be picked for a dangerous mission of poking around in the badlands looking for a small army of *bandidos*. Steiner, on the other hand, was more realistic.

"What's the matter, Sergeant Garrity?" he asked, walking over to the horse pickets. "Don't they expect us to come back?"

"Are you worried, Steiner?" Garrity asked.

Steiner shrugged. "I've been in the army seven years, Sergeant Garrity. I'm here because on the outside I was a disgrace to my family and myself. Whiskey dominates my life, which means I live in hell. If some border desperado puts a bullet in my skull, he'll be doing both me and the world a favor."

"In that case, you ride ahead of us on point,"

233

Garrity said. "I'd prefer to live long enough to spend years and years living on my army pension. Young Mauson still has to decide what he's going to do with his life, but I'm sure he wants a long one too. Since you don't give a damn about your survival, I don't either."

Steiner smiled. "Sure. I'll take the point."

Mauson, waiting for them at the horses, was already mounted. "How far are we gonna go, Sergeant?"

"Far enough to find some *bandidos,*" Garrity said.

Mauson patted the butt of his carbine. "I'm ready. They shot my bunky. I owe 'em one, that's for sure."

"I have a reason for revenge too," Steiner said. "If it wasn't for those bastards, I'd still be lying drunk in the ambulance."

The little patrol rode out of the camp. Steiner, following Garrity's orders, led them on a straight southeast course. They had only to go a short distance when the sergeant called a halt. He galloped up to Steiner.

"Are you blind?"

Steiner looked over at the N.C.O. "What's the matter?"

"Can't you see that smoke over there?" He pointed to an area where some low-lying hills broke the straightness of the horizon.

"I guess I wasn't looking," Steiner said lamely.

Garrity reached over and grabbed him by the collar, shaking him violently. "That's what I put you up on the point for. You're supposed to see that stuff before we do."

Steiner laughed. "You see, Sergeant? I'm even a failure at that simple job."

"You sonofabitch!" Garrity snarled. He motioned back to Mauson. "Come on up here." When the trooper joined them, he told the two what he wanted to do. "We'll ride over toward those foothills. We don't have the time or the circumstances to be sneaky, so we'll have to get in and out quick. We want to take a look at 'em and see what we're facing up to. Notice how many there are. Keep that in mind, because there's a good chance we all ain't gonna make it back."

Mauson's eyes opened a bit wide, but Steiner didn't seem particularly concerned.

Garrity, now leading the way, took them on a direct route toward their destination. They rode easily, keeping a lookout for any ambushes or attacks coming at them from the distance. But the Llano Estacado remained empty. When the patrol reached the base of the small rises, they went straight up to the nearest ridgeline and reined in.

The bandit camp was spread along a narrow draw that ran into the next hill. The outlaws were at ease, lounging around numerous campfires.

Garrity made a quick count. "I figure we've got a couple of dozen down there."

Steiner agreed. "They outnumber our little force about two to one."

Mauson reached over and tapped Garrity on the shoulder. "Look down there, Sergeant. I think a couple of 'em have spotted us."

Garrity glanced in the direction indicated. He saw two of the desperados pointing and gesturing to the others. "Yeah. I'd say the sonofbitches see our happy faces. Let's get the hell out of here."

They needed no further orders. The patrol made a rapid withdrawal, galloping down the hill to level ground, then letting the horses go all out.

They were able to go a full mile before Garrity saw the group coming in to intercept them from the right front. He signaled for Steiner and Mauson to follow as he turned off to the left. The bandits also cut their angle, making the point of contact even shorter.

Garrity, desperate, saw that there were seven after them. The more he turned away, the farther he got from the wagon train. If the present situation continued, the patrol would be completely cut off, giving the bandits the opportunity to massacre them at their leisure.

Even Mauson, for all his inexperience, could see what was going on. Steiner rode as calmly as possible aboard the speeding horse. He seemed to be concentrating on something else as they fled for their lives. Suddenly he gestured at Garrity.

Garrity, puzzled, looked over to see what the ex-hospital steward wanted.

Steiner grinned and waved good-bye. "Now I'll show you what I'm good for." He pulled his carbine from its boot and turned to ride straight at the bandits. He cocked the weapon and aimed as best he could. It was awkward shoving the next round into the chamber, but Steiner managed. He fired once more, the gap between himself and the pursuers rapidly closing.

Garrity wasted neither time nor sympathy. He swung back on a straight course toward the wagon train. With Mauson trailing him, the sergeant galloped across the Llano Estacado. After ten minutes he sighted the wagon train. Urging his horse on, he quickly covered the ground and rode within the circle of vehicles, coming to a halt so quickly that Mauson almost rode into him.

Wildon and Mulvaney rushed to the sergeant. "Looks like you found something."

"Yes, sir. There's a couple of dozen of 'em, sir. And I'd say they mean to pick a fight."

"Where is Steiner?" Wildon asked.

"Dying like a soldier right now unless they've already done him in." Garrity replied. "I'll make an official report."

"You'll have to wait," Wildon said. "Look."

The entire bandit gang appeared in the distance. Strung out, they came on slowly but persistently. Wildon alerted the men and ordered them to stand fast at their fighting stations. Hester and the other women huddled behind Dixie Mulvaney's large trunk.

Wildon, Garrity, and Mulvaney stood together watching the approaching enemy. The raiders had formed themselves into a single skirmish line, coming straight on.

"What do you think?" Wildon asked the two older sergeants.

"The first thing to take into consideration is that those sonofabitches are totally dedicated to the bandit chief," Garrity said. "His lukewarms have pulled out. All them crazies is just like that there colonel that called on us with the white flag."

"In other words they'll fight like hell," Wildon said.

Mulvaney agreed. "And they're making a straight-ahead military charge. I'd say they're going to try to bowl us over like cavalry normally would."

"I recall studying the Battle of Waterloo," Wildon said. "The British squares of infantry stood up to Napoleon's finest cavalry."

"Them English weren't outnumbered two-to-one," Garrity said. "And they weren't hurting for water on the Llano Estacado."

"They're moving in for the attack," Wildon

238

said.

"God help us," Mulvaney said calmly.

"If God won't, I'll settle for the devil in this case," Garrity said.

CHAPTER 22

The *bandidos'* battle line moved forward in an ominous manner. The border raiders began the opening maneuvers, keeping their horses to a walk. Then they broke into a canter, loping easily across the smooth, hard surface of the terrain. Finally a loud command could be heard shouted from the center of their formation.

"En avant! Al attaque!"

The desperado force broke into a full gallop, the hammering of their horses' hooves sounding like an avalanche.

Wildon had gotten all twelve of his men over to the side of their defense formation that faced the attackers. Each man had a round in his Springfield, ready to fire.

"Stand steady!" Wildon shouted.

The bandits cheered and began firing. Slugs slapped into the canvas tops of the wagons or banged into the wooden sides of the vehicles. A trooper suddenly collapsed at his post.

"Aim!"

Now bellowing, the border raiders stepped up their fire. Trooper John Jones, standing beside Gus Dortmann, grabbed his chest as he was spun completely around by the impact of a bullet. He hung onto a wagon wheel, then lost his grip and fell awkwardly to the ground.

"Fire!"

The army's volley blasted outward, and seven bandits tumbled from their saddles. Their companions swept on, charging in between the wagons, leaping over the hitching shafts and riding within the circle. They knew better than to try to stay there however, and they rode out the other side.

The soldiers on the line turned around and drew their pistols and fired rapidly at the enemy as they galloped back out into the desert.

One bandit, killed instantly, fell within the wagon train. Another pitched to the ground a dozen yards beyond it.

"Somebody gimme a hand," Dortmann yelled out. "Jones is hit."

Mauson and the teamster O'Leary helped Dortmann take Jones over to the surgeon's ambulance. Dempster was ready for casualties. "Put him up here, boys."

Hester Boothe and Dixie Mulvaney left the trunk and hurried to the impromptu hospital. "May we be of help, Doctor Dempster?" Hester asked.

"I'll let you know," Dempster said. He tore open Jones's shirt. A quick glance gave him all the information he needed. He shook his head.

Jones groaned. "God damn me! It hurts like hell."

"I can help that at least," Dempster said. He fetched a vial of morphine. Wetting his finger, he dabbed it in the powdery stuff and applied it directly inside Jones's massive wounds. It took several applications, but after a few moments, the injured man was more at ease.

Jones's breath was shallow and his face visibly blanched. "I ain't gonna make it."

"You're bleeding inside," Dempster said without making any denials of the injured trooper's true condition.

"I seen this in other fellers," Jones said weakly. "So it's come to me, has it?"

Hester, standing nearby, felt deep sympathy for the dying man. She walked up to the stretcher and placed her hand on his forehead.

He smiled up at her. "I heard you was a big help with Rampey, Missus Boothe. He said—" Jones coughed a bit. "He said you was a real comfort."

Dempster handed a damp rag to Hester. "That's all the water I can spare. It'll make him feel better."

Hester gently wiped his face. "You'll be all

right," she said.

Jones shook his head. "No, I won't. But it's most kind of you to say so." He began to have trouble breathing, but finally settled down a bit. "Missus Boothe?"

"Yes, Mister Jones?"

"When they bury me, tell 'em my real name, please."

Hester was shocked at how fast the man was sinking. She had been in the same room when her grandfather died, but he had succumbed to old age and went easily without pain. Jones's eyes looked as if they were glazing over. "I know your last name, but not your first, Mister Jones," she said.

"My real moniker is Francis Thompson," he said. "That's what I want on my marker." It was getting difficult for him to speak. "I 'listed—" He had to stop and rest. "I 'listed as Jones—got a bobtail discharge—last hitch. I had to lie—lie about who I was—to get back in the army." He managed a grin. "—couldn't make it—on the outside."

"Francis Thompson," Hester said. "I'll remember. Where and when were you born, Mister Thompson?" Hester noted he seemed to be staring off into space. "Mister Thompson?"

"He's gone," Dempster said.

While Trooper Francis Thompson alias John Jones was giving up the ghost, 2d Lt. Wildon

243

Boothe's mind was working hard at coming up with some tactical solution. He didn't have the slightest intention of letting the bandits slowly but surely wear them down. All he had to do was figure out a way to keep that from happening.

Aside from getting a good education at West Point, the academy's curriculum and customs taught him how to think fast on his feet. And that's exactly what was being required of the young officer at that particular time.

Wildon did not come up with the idea in any logical steps or processes. The entire concept leaped straight into his consciousness with all the subtlety of a cannonball hitting the side of a fortification.

"Sergeant Mulvaney!" he shouted. "Sergeant Garrity!"

The two N.C.O.s, standing on the defensive perimeter with the men, immediately hurried over to the wagon train's young commander. Wildon gave his instructions quickly, clearly, and precisely. When he had finished, the two N.C.O.s looked at each other.

"I don't think I've ever heard of anything like that," Mulvaney said.

"It's different," Garrity calmly allowed.

"Remember!" Wildon said. "It won't work unless all six cartridges in each man's revolver are loaded and there is a round chambered in the Springfields. See to it!"

"Yes, sir!"

"And make damned sure they don't fire until I say so," Wildon said. "By God, if any man fires before my orders, I'll nail his hide to the guardhouse wall. Got it!"

"Yes, sir!"

Wildon wisely let the two sergeants prepare the men. That was their job, and his was to direct the defense of the wagon train. Still tired after the awful episode of rescuing Hester, he was now damned good and angry.

The two sergeants had no sooner reported back to him, then the men shouted out the alarm. Wildon went to the line of defense. He could see the bandits appearing again.

Garrity spat. "I'd say that leader of theirs gave 'em one hell of a pep talk."

"Yeah?" Wildon said. "Then we'll give 'em one hell of a nasty surprise." He stepped back. "Are you ready?" he bellowed at the men."

"Yes, sir!" came the unanimous answer.

"Then stand fast," Wildon said. "I don't want one son of a bitch to so much as blink an eye unless I say so."

The bandits aligned themselves and began cantering as before. When their formation was tight and properly dressed and covered down in a tactical cavalry formation, the same voice cried out as before.

"En avant! Al ataque!"

Now thundering toward the wagon train, the bandit gang shouted wildly, leaning low over their horses' necks as they pressed on.

"Draw pistols!" Wildon shouted.

The men, holding their Springfields in their left hands, drew their pistols and held them with their right.

The border raiders came rapidly closer, firing spasmodically as they closed the gap.

"Hold it! Hold it!" Wildon cautioned his troops. "Damn your eyes! Wait for my command!"

Now the bandits were within fifteen yards. Pressed in close, their shock power promised to be devastating. Finally they reached the soldiers and charged within the wagons.

"Fire!" Wildon bellowed. *"Fire! Fire!"*

Every man raised his pistol into the close targets and fired six shots. The sixty bullets hit human and horse flesh both. Men and animals spun and crashed to the ground in the awful, continuous thunder of the Colt pistols.

Now the troopers raised the carbines, firing the single, heavy .45-caliber bullets into the few surviving bandits. The area between the wagons was filled with fallen men and horses.

The soldiers now charged the living outlaws, in hand-to-hand battle with carbine butts, knives, and even fists and boots. Many of the troops had the presence of mind to pick up pistols and rifles from fallen raiders. The shock of the heavy casualties and this extra firepower pressed hard on the surviving outlaws.

Wildon saw one man, tall and gaunt as Hester had described him, in the center of the melee. Quickly shoving three rounds into his revolver's cylinder, he rushed toward the *bandido*.

Mauveaux could see the man running toward him was an officer by the shoulder straps he wore. He also knew who it was. "Ah!" he cried out. *"C'est une affaire d'honneur, monsieur!"* Snarling, he raised his pistol to shoot.

Wildon quickly dropped to one knee and brought his revolver up. He squeezed off all three rounds. One hit Mauveaux's torso, making him jump back crazily. The second slammed into the Frenchman's head and dumped him onto his back. The third flew off into the sky above the Llano Estacado.

Gradually the roar of the battle simmered down until complete silence covered the scene. A few surviving bandits, who had been lucky enough not to be caught in the roaring fusillade, galloped away in an unorganized rout toward Mexico.

Stunned but thankful it was over, the troopers and the women looked at the carnage around them. No one moved for several moments until Sergeant Garrity walked up to Wildon.

"Sir," he said saluting. "Two men dead, three wounded, and two present for duty."

Wildon took a deep breath. "Well, Sergeant, it looks like you and I will be driving wagons the rest of the way to Fort Mojave."

CHAPTER 23

Reveille was sounded at Fort Mojave, Arizona Territory. The persistent notes swept over the post from Soap Suds Row up to the officers' quarters.

Second Lieutenant Wildon Boothe, as usual, responded instinctively to the call. He sat up before he was fully awake and did not open his eyes until his feet were on the floor. But instead of being asleep in bed, he was dozing in a chair in the regimental headquarters. Detailed as the officer of the day, he had been on duty all night. He stood up and stretched. As soon as Reveille was over, he would be relieved from any more responsibility for the rest of the day.

The wagon train had arrived more than a month before. After the survivors had buried their dead — which included a proper marker for Trooper "John Jones" — and left the hated bandits to mummify in the desert sun or be eaten by vultures, the small group had traveled unmolested to their destination.

The regimental sergeant major stepped in

through the front door. "Good morning to you, sir," the senior N.C.O. said.

"I'm happy to see you," Wildon said gratefully. "Tell the adjutant there is nothing unusual to report."

"No fights in the barracks or sutler's last night, sir?"

"Not even a shout," Wildon said. "I'll see you later, Sergeant." He went outside and walked toward his quarters on officers' row.

When he entered his small house, a delicious odor wafted into the room from the kitchen. Wildon strolled through the bed chamber and into the cooking area. The cast-iron quartermaster stove had a dancing fire in it. A pot of coffee bubbled on it. Hester looked up from the skillet that splattered with frying bacon.

"K Troop slaughtered a pig yesterday," she said. "Mary Dougherty saved us some of the bacon."

Wildon poured himself a cup of coffee. He took a cautious sip, then a healthy gulp. "This tastes wonderful."

"You sound surprised," Hester said.

"I am," he said in all candor.

"Dixie told me the best way to prepare army-issue coffee," Hester said.

"Did Mary teach you how to fry bacon?"

"She gave me some helpful hints," Hester said. "I'm afraid there are no eggs, but the bacon will be a welcome change to salt pork, won't it?" She

250

pointed to the mirror on the wall where a basin of hot water sat. "Everything is ready for your morning shave."

Wildon smiled. "You're quite the army wife, aren't you?"

"I'm learning."

Wildon stripped off his tunic, and picked up his shaving mug. After lathering his face, he began to slowly strop his razor. "Hester."

"Yes, darling?"

"I have written out my resignation," Wildon said. "I'll submit it to the regimental adjutant tomorrow morning."

Hester stopped cooking and looked over at him.

"Of course it will take a little time for it to be processed," he said. "And we have to make arrangements for transport back to New York." He began to shave. "I think I'll pass up the chance for a job with Bristol Soap, however. My own family can arrange a suitable position."

Hester finished the bacon and put it out on the plates. "Wildon, why are you doing this?"

"I've been terribly selfish, darling," Wildon said. He carefully ran the razor under his chin. "I had no right to ask you to endure all this."

"Endure this?" She laughed. "Wildon, some of my dearest friends in the world live here. Dixie Mulvaney, Mary Dougherty, and even Elisa Abernathy." She looked at him. "Darling, after

251

just six months behind a desk in a brokerage house, you would be stark raving mad."

"Maybe not," he said.

"Wildon, I saw what kind of a man you are out there on the desert," Hester said. "You are a born soldier. You belong here, and I want to be by your side."

He turned and looked at her. "Do you really mean that?"

"My sweet husband, I love you with all my heart. I would much rather live with you here than put up with you back in New York," Hester said. "Your company would be impossible to endure."

Wildon wiped the remaining lather from his face. He turned and looked at her. "Hester—"

A knock at the door sounded. Hester walked over and opened it. Sergeant Garrity tipped his kepi. "Some o' the men would like to speak to you, ma'am," he said. "It seemed all right so I brung 'em over." He motioned to the soldiers with him.

Several troopers stood there, including Harold Rampey who still sported a sling. "Good morning, Missus Boothe." He saw Wildon and saluted. "Good morning, sir."

Puzzled, Wildon walked to the door. "What can we do for you men?"

"We got something for Missus Boothe," Rampey said.

"We made it ourselves," his friend David Mauson added.

"It was for the way she watched out for us with the surgeon," Gus Dortmann added. He had suffered a painful thigh wound during the final charge of the bandits. "We know how hard it is to get good furniture."

"What have you got there?" Hester asked, smiling.

"It's a little dressing table, ma'am," Dortmann said. "We made it out of hardtack boxes. Can we bring it in?"

"Certainly," Wildon said.

"Oh, look!" Hester exclaimed. "It's got a mirror on it. Where in the world did you get that?"

"We all chipped in and bought it at the sutler's ma'am," Rampey said. He and Mauson carried it in and set it down in the kitchen. "We don't especially like the color, but it was the only kind o' paint we could steal—"

Sergeant Garrity interrupted. "He means draw outta quartermaster stores."

"I think blue is lovely," Hester said. "Thank you so much."

"It's got a drawer in it, see?" Mauson said. He demonstrated it. "You can put stuff in it, if you'd like."

"Thank you so much," Hester said beaming. "I love it. You are all so kind to have gone to such trouble." She walked up to the cleverly constructed table. "It's wonderfully smooth to the touch!"

"We sanded it down, ma'am," Harold Rampey explained.

"Give her the card, Rampey," Garrity said.

"We all signed this sentiment, ma'am," the young trooper said, handing it over.

Smiling with delight, Hester took the envelope and opened it. The message was short, but there were more than a dozen signatures and a couple of "X's" beside which someone else had written the names.

To Mrs. Boothe,
   We wish to express our gratitude for the kindness and consideration you showed us soldiers. As far as we are concerned, you are the First Lady of the Regiment.

"How sweet!" Hester said. "Oh dear, how thoughtless of me. Would you like some coffee?"

"If it's no trouble, ma'am," Dortmann said.

"It's no trouble at all," Hester said. "Please sit down. I believe we have enough cups now."

"Do you suppose I might have another too," Wildon said.

"Of course, dear," Hester said. She walked over to the stove to get the coffeepot. "Oh, Wildon."

"Yes?"

"I don't think it's necessary for you to see the

adjutant, do you?"

"Not if you say so," he replied happily.

"I do say so," Hester said. She laughed. "Be it ever so humble—"

"—there's no place like the U.S. Cavalry," Wildon added with a smile.

Hester laughed and served the coffee. As her unexpected guests enjoyed the hot brew, she went over to the dressing table to give it a careful examination.

It was the most beautiful piece of furniture she had ever owned—and that included the expensive pieces back in New York.

POWELL'S ARMY
BY TERENCE DUNCAN

#1: UNCHAINED LIGHTNING   (1994, $2.50)
Thundering out of the past, a trio of deadly enforcers dispenses its own brand of frontier justice throughout the untamed American West! Two men and one woman, they are the U.S. Army's most lethal secret weapon—they are POWELL'S ARMY!

#2: APACHE RAIDERS   (2073, $2.50)
The disappearance of seventeen Apache maidens brings tribal unrest to the violent breaking point. To prevent an explosion of bloodshed, Powell's Army races through a nightmare world south of the border—and into the deadly clutches of a vicious band of Mexican flesh merchants!

#3: MUSTANG WARRIORS   (2171, $2.50)
Someone is selling cavalry guns and horses to the Comanche—and that spells trouble for the bluecoats' campaign against Chief Quanah Parker's bloodthirsty Kwahadi warriors. But Powell's Army are no strangers to trouble. When the showdown comes, they'll be ready—and someone is going to die!

#4: ROBBERS ROOST   (2285, $2.50)
After hijacking an army payroll wagon and killing the troopers riding guard, Three-Fingered Jack and his gang high-tail it into Virginia City to spend their ill-gotten gains. But Powell's Army plans to apprehend the murderous hardcases before the local vigilantes do—to make sure that Jack and his slimy band stretch hemp the legal way!